I0532651

FROM THINE OWN WELL

Norm Hamilton

Cover design by Elliot of Hamilton Boucher Media Inc.
Book Design and Production by Meldrum House Publishing
Editing by Erin Potter, Shamrock Editing

Norm Hamilton

Library and Archives Canada Cataloguing in Publication

Hamilton, Norm, 1951-, author
    From thine own well / written by Norm Hamilton.

Issued in print and electronic formats.
ISBN 978-0-9918315-3-1 (pbk.).--ISBN 978-0-9918315-4-8 (kindle).--
ISBN 978-0-9918315-5-5 (epub)

    I. Title.

PS8615.A4426F76 2013   C813'.6   C2013-907729-4
                                         C2013-907730-8

Meldrum
HOUSE
publishing

ISBN-10: 0991831535
Paperback ISBN: 9780991831531
ebook epub ISBN: 9780991831555
Kindle eBook ISBN: 9780991831548
www.normhamilton.ca

Table of Contents

Norm Hamilton

To Anna: My muse, critic, love and best friend

For my children and their spouses, Jenny, Becky, Elliot and Alain: Thank you for your support and love.

Thanks also to Damien Tremblay for his encouragement, support and proofreading.

§§§

Drink waters out of thine own cistern, and running waters out of thine own well.
Proverbs 5:15

If we pollute the air, water and soil that keep us alive and well, and destroy the biodiversity that allows natural systems to function, no amount of money will save us.
David Suzuki

Henry Kissinger is reported to have stated, "Yes, many people will die when the New World Order is established, but it will be a much better world for those who survive".
Kissinger was wrong...at least on the second point

iv

Prologue

Canada's democracy has succumbed to corporatism. What is to become of the country? Only God knows for sure.

In the fall of 2012, the Government of Canada entered into a 31-year agreement with Chinese government-owned business interests that gave their corporations the right to sue the Government of Canada and other levels of governments if enactments were put in place by any at any level that interfered with their profits. This effectively released those corporations from the restrictions of Canadian law or environmental concerns.

That history-altering document became known as *The Agreement*. It set the stage for further covenants and heralded the most deleterious epoch in Canadian history.

The foreign conglomerates were not compelled to comply with environmental requirements, labour legislation or regulations. Existing Canadian mining, gas and oil exploration companies could no longer compete in their own country. Agreements between the Yukon government and Chinese corporations allowed the majority rights to the mineral, gas and oil resources through Yukon to be sold off. This included huge areas such as the Peel Watershed in northeastern Yukon and the Tintina Trench which ran in a diagonal line from Southwest Yukon northwesterly to the Alaska border as well as south into Alberta.

Hydraulic Fracturing (Fracking), a process for extracting oil and gas, began in earnest in 2014 and contaminated the water in the entire southern portion of Yukon. Within 10 years the numbers of wildlife, birds and fish had diminished to a point of scarcity—hundreds of

Yukoners died from poisoning before it became apparent that it was the adulterated water table that was the problem.

The collection of fresh water was made illegal. An order was made that all water must be purchased only through those who were licensed by a corporate cartel known as The Coalition for Citizens' Benefit (The Coalition); ostensibly to protect the public from water adulterated with noxious substances but also serving to pad the coffers of The Coalition. Agriculture and animal husbandry were outlawed due to the contamination of the soil and feed.

The pristine wilderness of Yukon had been sullied.

Government employees (public servants), their numbers decimated by death and layoffs, had become complicit in the enforcement of the rules in order to keep their jobs.

Whitehorse, the Capital of Yukon, a city once boasting a population of over 30,000 including the surrounding area, became a virtual ghost town with fewer than 10,000 remaining. Thousands fled from the area hoping to circumvent the devastation that had come with the poisoning of the water and lowering of the water table only to find the wanton destruction of resources and environment was happening nation-wide. The road between Whitehorse and Dawson City was maintained only to the point where the trucks and equipment for the mining operations could turn off to go into the Ogilvie Mountain area and continue the ravaging of the ecosystem there in order to satisfy the corporate demands for the resources.

Yukon's 30-year policing agreement with the Royal Canadian Mounted Police (RCMP) expired in 2032. The once renowned police force had lost credibility and prestige due to internal difficulties which culminated in the creation of a television reality show. The RCMP was replaced by The Coalition's own militia for the enforcement of rules and regulations that The Coalition created or approved. The militia answered only to them. The RCMP was reduced to a few detectives who continued to serve only as police for the federal government in respect to Criminal Code matters.

In 2034 the Government of Canada was effectively bankrupted. A decision by an international arbitration panel had awarded a series of damages to The Coalition which was quickly successful in taking control of the nation and her people. The majority of Canadian citizens remained compliant to those who ruled them and apathetic toward change. Elections became a thing of the past and governments were appointed by the ruling corporatist elite.

However, not everyone stood by in fear. In each area of the country there were small factions who were willing to stand against the tyranny, ready to put themselves on the line. For most of them it was a series of personal experiences that brought them together. One of those small groups lived in Yukon and, like other like-minded groups, focused their efforts to regain sovereignty over Canada.

For The Coalition, it was imperative to stop them.

The year is 2036.

Norm Hamilton

Chapter 1

The vastness west of Whitehorse was bathed in a golden glow as the sun rose over McIntyre Mountain. No stirring of animals or ruffling of birds signalled the beginning of the day; there hadn't been any for over 15 years. Landon McGuire grunted as he rolled over on the makeshift bunk in his cabin at the south end of Coal Lake. He squinted against the blazing sunlight that flooded the single window beside the wooden slab door. The smell of the rough-sawn plank floor permeated the air and dust particles sparkled in the glowing rays that streamed through the chinks in the walls. The 45-gallon drum wood stove in the corner had seen better days as a pile of fine ashes dribbled on the floor beneath its door.

He swung his legs over the side of the bed and pushed his six-foot frame to a sitting position. His head ached from the effort to drown his memories with home-distilled spruce gin. *Gawd*, he thought, *my mouth tastes like sap*. Breakfast was out of the question. After pulling his greying hair back and securing it into a pony-tail with an elastic band, he scoured the floor for his clothes.

His mind wandered back to the years he'd worked in mining exploration, spending weeks at a time in the wilderness staking claims. It had been a wonderful period in his life; time outdoors and Wenda waiting at home when he came back. He remembered the mines taking pains to ensure they caused as little interference to the environment as was humanly possible.

Then it had all changed. After *The Agreement*, the mining industry got careless in their approach to resource

1

extraction. He became saddened and ashamed to be a part of it. His sadness had turned to despair when Wenda died. It was then that he had quit and moved to the cabin. He still questioned if the carelessness of the mines or oil and gas companies had contributed to her death. Since then, he'd sought solace as a recluse and had as little to do with other people as possible.

A scratching on the floor from beneath the mattress interrupted his thoughts and announced the awakening of his husky-shepherd cross dog, Bob. Landon interrupted his search to watch as Bob stretched, pointing one hind leg at a time behind him. Then, ears up and tail switching back and forth, he wiggled his white and black body over to Landon.

"What d'ya think, Bob? Should we head out to the horseshoe?" His question was met with a vigorously wagging tail. Landon was planning a hike to a hidden location where he could collect fresh water without having to purchase it from The Coalition.

His eyes took in the cabin—spartan, but always kept clean and tidy. Wenda had always insisted their home be spotless. A cracked mirror on the wash stand reflected a day's growth of stubble on his leathered face that he decided could wait another day. He pulled on an old pair of blue jeans and shoved his socked feet into a pair of well-worn boots. The early August sun beat down on the cabin as he stuffed a warm fleece and waterproof jacket into a backpack in preparation for the drop in temperature during the hike into the mountains.

Things have sure changed, he thought as he strapped a 44-magnum around his waist and slid a pair of throwing knives into sleeves prepared for them on his bandoleer. He could remember when there was no need for weapons other than a rifle in case of bears. Now, with the water situation, it was desperate people that were of more concern. After slinging a .308 calibre Winchester over his right shoulder, he headed out the door with Bob following close behind.

As soon as they were in the open, Landon stopped to listen, peering in all directions, looking for any indication of others. Satisfied that no one was around, he grabbed the handle of the cart with the empty water vessels and struck off on the 14-kilometre trek to the crescent-shaped bowl west of his cabin near Coal Lake that had been formed by the Ibex volcano in some distant past.

Clean water was no longer readily available as it was in the days before *The Agreement*. Even the water near his cabin was suspect. They were headed for one of the few spots left where the water ran clean and pure.

Landon smiled, noticing the forest trail was showing signs of lack of use as the vegetation began to overgrow it. He always liked it when nature reclaimed its space. As they walked, Landon kept an eye on Bob, watching for any reactions to their surroundings. The dog could feel, instinctively, when someone, or something, was near.

Kirsten settled back into the wooden corner bench of the coffee shop so she could see the sidewalk on Main Street but would still have a solid wall at her back. Her backpack rested on the floor between her sneaker-covered feet while she cupped her latte in both hands and stared at the chocolate swirl in the cream. Her only other apparel was a floor-length, loose fitting cotton dress. As always, her Virtual Portable Computer (VPC), was within reach on the table, its keyboard visible on the opened hardware, the hologram screen turned off for the moment. A brown envelope rested on top of the keys.

She sat, twirling her blond hair in her fingers, her eyes circling around the bistro. The envelope came into her peripheral vision and she quickly turned away, and then focused on it. Her right hand inched forward, tentatively caressing the tawny paper and drawing it slowly forward. She picked it up and examined it. The answer she had been waiting for, the response from *Macleod's Magazine* to her submitted article on the political landscape in Yukon, waited inside.

Her left index finger dug under the flap of the envelope, tearing it open painstakingly slow. The letter was revealed and she began reading. "Dear Ms. Allerton," it began, "Thank you for your submission to *Macleod's Magazine*. Unfortunately, the piece that you have sent does not fit with our editorial requirements at this time." She read no further; she had seen enough rejection letters in her short twenty-five years. It had been five years since she'd finished journalism school in Toronto and she hadn't managed to get any articles published that were not favourable to the government or The Coalition.

Frustrated, she ripped it in half, then tore it again as she stepped around the corner to drop it into the trash. She realized that her backpack and VPC were unattended and turned on her heel to return to her seat. Her eyes filled with tears as she gazed out the window, oblivious to the pedestrian traffic that flowed down the Main Street sidewalk.

She tossed her VPC into her backpack and stormed out of the coffee shop, headed on a direct path across Front Street, past the White Pass Train Station to the embankment overlooking the Yukon River. She stared at the flowing water, her eyes unfocused, her mind a flurry of thoughts and questions. She wondered, *why won't the mainstream press print anything that doesn't support government?* She skidded down the bank toward the glacier-fed waters. *What's the point in trying to get information out there?*

She set her backpack on the large rocks beside the Whitehorse Wharf and sat down to unfold her VPC. She started drafting a new article, questioning why it was so difficult to get information published. Disheartened, Kirsten slammed her VPC closed and threw it into her backpack, leaving it on the rocks as she stood up stiffly, facing the water, not noticing the light rain that was falling. She wanted to scream.

"I sure hope you're not intending on jumping in?" came a voice from her left.

Kirsten jumped, startled; her left foot slid off the rocks and she lost her balance and fell backward. She rolled quickly toward the sound of the voice, prepared to defend herself. The high cheek-boned smiling face of a young First Nations man looked back at her from the shadows under the wharf. She scrambled to her feet and grabbed at her pack and VPC. *Oh, shit, what have I gotten into*, she asked herself as she scowled at him.

"Jesus. You scared the shit out of me, you asshole," she said, clutching her belongings. "What the hell do you think you're doing?" She was immediately sorry for her outburst and glanced around for the quickest escape route.

"Hopefully stopping you from doing something foolish," he said softly.

"What are you talking about? Who are you?" she asked. "And why are you hiding under the wharf?"

She watched as he crawled out from under the concrete and stood facing her from about 7 metres away, a hand slid into one pocket. He was dressed in blue jeans and a t-shirt with a pair of solid-looking hiking boots.

"Folks just call me Stone," he answered quietly. That had been John Stone's moniker since his family moved from Old Crow to Whitehorse when he was an infant twenty-nine years earlier.

He took a step toward her, balancing himself carefully on the huge boulders. She took a step backward and slipped, dropping her things. Stone leaped forward, catching her before she went down. He slid his arm around her waist and held her steady. She pulled away, her eyes wary.

"I think it's best we get off these rocks," he said. "You want me to grab your stuff?"

Kirsten shook her head as she stooped to pick up her possessions and then gingerly stepped down from the rocks onto the sandy bank beside them, a short distance from the wharf. Stone stepped off the rocks and stood a couple of metres away, facing her.

"You didn't tell me what you're doing under there," she said as she connected with his smiling brown eyes.

"It's dry and quiet. Well, it's usually quiet," he smiled. "I've been coming to the wharf since we moved here when I was a kid. Were you really thinking of jumping in?"

"No, but I damn near fell in when you showed up," she said. "I thought I'd get some peace by watching the water flow by."

Quietness overcame them as they stood on the riverbank facing the water.

"I remember when the salmon used to run in this river," said Stone after a while. "At one time they were here by the thousands, then only by the hundreds and now so few they don't even bother counting them."

"What happened to them?"

"It was overfishing, initially. But then something happened to the water and it was like they couldn't find their way back. Salmon have to find their way back to where they were hatched in order to spawn." He had spent an entire summer studying the decline of the salmon population on his way to a B.Sc. in environmental science.

Stone moved closer to the water's edge and motioned along the bank with his hand. "See how far back the bushes are. Even the vegetation doesn't do well around this river anymore."

Kirsten stepped nearer the river and stood beside him. The motion of the water flowing by mesmerized them into a state of calm. Kirsten leaned forward and pointed into the water.

"Where do you think that came from?" she asked as an oil slick, appearing seemingly out of nowhere, undulated past on the surface of the water.

"Who knows?" Stone said. "There's a number of creeks between here and Marsh Lake, so it could have come from one of them. Or maybe someone dumped something into the river up at the old Robert Service Campground. No one's looked after that for a long time now."

Kirsten sat on a rock and turned to Stone. "Why did you mention the creeks?" she asked. "Are they that polluted?" Was this a story in the making, she wondered?

He moved closer and sat beside her. "Not usually. But if someone disturbed the ground upstream, I guess they could cause an old spill of some kind to get into the water. Heck, maybe there's someone mining up one of them," he laughed.

"Is that possible?" she asked. "Could there be a mine somewhere that is polluting this river? This is the only water left in Yukon that is supposed to be protected from this kind of thing." She was thinking of the amendments to the *Navigation Protection Act* that she had researched for an article a number of years earlier that had removed environmental protection from the majority of waters in Canada.

Stone's brow furrowed as he thought about her question. During his studies in environmental science he had researched the effect that careless mining had on the surrounding watersheds. "You could always go to the Mining Recorder Office and see if there's any mines registered around here," he suggested. "I'd be happy to come with you, if you'd like. You've got my curiosity up as well."

Kirsten locked eyes with him. She was hesitant to get involved with a total stranger, but the prospect of finding a source of pollution to a protected water system excited her. What a coup that would be. They'd have to publish that, she thought. "How about first thing Monday morning?" she replied.

Dust and rocks catapulted into the air as Paddy ground into third gear and wrestled the old Sportage around the next corner. Gwen leaned forward against her seatbelt and clutched the dashboard, staring straight ahead. Keira, 6, and Aaron, 12, laughed as they were jostled in the backseat. The air behind them reeked of burnt oil as the slick tires struggled to maintain purchase on the gravel road. The Doyles were on their way to experience some wilderness.

"That was the north end of Fish Lake we just passed," Paddy called back to the kids. "Let's find a place to park and get out and start hiking?" A short distance more, the road ended and he could go no further. He and the kids bailed out of the SUV and started checking out their surroundings. Gwen sat firm in her seat, her saucer-like eyes riveted toward the forest before her.

Paddy pulled the backpack they had brought with them from behind the back seat and then ambled around to the passenger side and tapped lightly on the window. The door handle had been useless for months. "Roll the window down," he coaxed.

Gwen eased herself back in the seat and slowly turned her head toward him. He grinned and tapped again. She leaned forward and grasped the window crank and gradually rolled down the window.

"It's great here. Are you coming out?" Paddy said.

Gwen was uneasy. "I don't think this is such a good idea, Paddy. We really don't know what we're doing and this old car isn't safe. I'm scared."

Paddy reached inside through the open window to open the door with the interior handle. As it opened he leaned in and gave Gwen a kiss on the cheek and a light hug. He loved the way the sunlight highlighted the red tones of her auburn hair.

"Aw, it'll be OK," he said. "We're not going very far and it's not that many kilometres back to town. Come on, it'll be fun."

Gwen raised her eyebrows at him. Then she smiled and accepted his outstretched hand as she slid off the seat and placed her flip-flops into the dirt. They hugged again

9

and stared into the forest and up the trail they would follow. Gwen turned around and checked behind them.

"Where's the kids?" she asked.

"They can't be very far, we just got here," Paddy said. "Keira! Aaron! Get back here. You're scaring your mother."

A giggle from the other side of the Kia gave away the children's hiding spot. Paddy winked at Gwen, and started around the vehicle toward the front. Gwen went the other way. Everybody laughed as they converged and grabbed the kids, tickling and wrestling with them.

"OK, everyone, let's head up the trail," said Paddy.

He grabbed the pack of food and drinks and led the way up the narrow path. Aaron clamoured along behind him, trying to place his sandal-clad feet in his father's footsteps. Keira and Gwen brought up the rear, relaxed and happy in their new summer frocks.

After a couple of hours of stepping over fallen logs, slipping on large stones, but continuing their trek up the hillside, they found themselves at a fork in the road. By that time they had reached the far end of Fish Lake and were beginning to get tired. The trail expanded into a small clearing in the bush.

"Let's take a break and have some lunch," Paddy said. "We've brought some really great stuff."

Gwen helped pull the pack down from his shoulders, and then opened it to take out their picnic. She spread a blanket on the ground and laid the containers of fried chicken, potato salad and cookies on the blanket. She took two large bottles of soft drinks out, opened one, and drained it into glasses. She watched lovingly as her children devoured their meal. After the long walk and a large meal they found themselves pleasantly full and tired.

"Maybe we can just stay here for a while and take a break," said Gwen.

"Great idea. What do you guys think?" Paddy asked the kids.

"Aw, let's keep going," called Aaron from inside the bush where he had gone to urinate. "I want to see more."

"I'm tired," said Keira as her eyelids became heavier.

"It's settled then. We'll take a little break and then go a little bit farther," said Paddy. Aaron scrunched his face, but settled into a quiet space beside his dad. In a few minutes he was sound asleep. Keira curled her body and rested her head on Gwen's lap and was soon snoring softly. Gwen stroked her copper tresses. Paddy and Gwen smiled quietly at each other as they watched their kids sleep.

An hour later they were on their way again. They hiked another kilometre and found a creek flowing across the path. Gwen bent to pick Keira up and carry her over the water. *That's odd that this path goes through a creek*, she thought as she studied the flow. She wondered if the stream had always been there. When she got to the other side she set Keira down and continued up the path. After a few steps she glanced back to see Keira kneeling at the stream's edge, scooping water into her hands and drinking it.

"Don't drink that," Gwen called to her. "I'll give you some from our water bottle."

"But it tastes good, Mommy... and it's cold," Keira smiled.

Gwen laughed. "I know it does, Honey, but it might not be safe; remember we are only to drink water we buy. Come on, catch up. Let's get going. Daddy and Aaron are getting way ahead of us."

11

They started up the trail, calling ahead to let the others know they were coming; all the while they could hear Paddy and Aaron laughing and talking to each other. Another half-hour lapsed before Keira began to lag behind.

"Come on Keira, we have to catch up," encouraged Gwen.

"I'm not feeling very well Mommy. I feel dizzy and my tummy hurts. My tummy really hurts."

Gwen frowned, but kept moving forward. She froze a few minutes later when Keira stopped in her tracks, and then sat down. "Mommy it really hurts." She lay on her side, drawing her knees to her chest and began sobbing.

"Keira! What's going on? What's wrong?"

"My tummy hurts so bad. And I'm so thirsty."

"Paddy!" screamed Gwen. "Get back here! Something's wrong with Keira!"

Paddy and Aaron wheeled around and ran back. They had stepped over a couple of fallen trees on the path and now leaped over them in their haste. Paddy slipped and fell forward onto a downed tree. A broken branch punctured his right shoulder and blood oozed out onto his cotton shirt. He scampered to his feet and kept running back to Gwen and Keira.

"What happened? What's wrong with her?" he asked, breathless.

"I don't know. She says she's sick and now her tummy is sore," said Gwen. "I don't know what to do. We have to get back home." She turned to Paddy and saw the bloodstain on his shoulder. "My God, what happened to you?"

"It's nothing. I slipped and fell. Let's get back to the car." Paddy knelt and scooped Keira into his arms,

12

supporting her weight with his left arm while favouring his right. He stood, panicked, his eyes darting around the bush.

"I think it will be quicker if we just cut straight across instead of following the trail," he said. "A straight line is always shorter than a crooked one. Let's go."

They charged into the forest with Paddy leading the way back to the car. Aaron began to cry as he ran; confusion and fear overtaking him. Gwen moved swiftly behind him, reassuring and consoling him as they struggled to keep up with Paddy.

Paddy dropped his eyes from the trail to his daughter's face as he felt her go limp in his arms. He stumbled to his knees, then dragged himself erect again to struggle up the next hill. *We have to get to the car soon*, he thought.

Chapter 2

Wolfgang Grimm smiled as he ran his finger across the gold-embossed nameplate on the solid oak door to his office. *President, Yukon Division of The Coalition for Citizens Benefit* it read. He pushed down on the ivory inlaid golden handle and walked through. The room covered half the top floor of the Main Street building in Whitehorse that had been previously renovated for visiting government ministers. Of course, that was when there were still elected governments. Resplendent with solid oak wall coverings and luxurious bison hide furniture, the office screamed of power.

He relaxed into an oversize presidential-style chair behind a substantial teak desk. It was custom built for him to compensate for his diminutive stature and gave the appearance of size and strength to his visitors. Two simple, wooden chairs sat directly in front of the desk. To the right stood a glass-topped bar that was fully stocked with various types of liquor, brandy, scotch and wine. On the left a gathering of couches sat in a circle for entertaining guests. A cooler stocked with imported meats, fruits and vegetables completed the display.

Leaning forward, he placed his thumb on the print recognition pad at the front of the desktop and grinned as a holograph screen instantly appeared in front of him. "Welcome to your Virtual Desktop," the built-in speakers announced. This latest technology included complete voice activation and control with a virtual keyboard available for those times when quiet input was preferred. From the other side of the desk, it appeared like nothing was there.

At the far end, enclosed in glass walls, was a huge conference table that measured 3 metres by 8 metres. Plush, fabric-covered chairs surrounded the table. An air-conditioning system delivered filtered, heated or appropriately cooled air into the entire office area.

A light tapping at his door brought his mind back to the present. Mahalia, a Bahamian-Canadian woman in her early 40's he'd hired as his personal secretary and executive assistant, appeared in the door jamb. The Mulatto woman intrigued him. She used no family name—just Mahalia. He found her irresistible.

"Good morning, Sir," she began. "The Vice-Pres..."

His eyes wandered to the curve of her calf where it met the hem of her business suit.

"Sorry. What was that, Mahalia? I wasn't paying attention."

"The Vice President of the Department of Peace and Well Being is here to see you, Sir. He's in the waiting room."

"Any idea what the hell he wants?" *Jesus, that guy has been a pain ever since he got here,* he thought. *Why did they bring someone in from China?*

"Something about a Resistance, a push-back. People not doing what they're told."

"Okay. Show the son of a bitch in."

Mahalia tossed her midnight black hair as she turned to leave. He was riveted on her form-fitted suit as it hugged her curves perfectly, and was particularly attracted to her legs and four-inch heels. He rose from behind his desk, and then straightened his tie and smoothed his designer suit jacket before striding behind the bar. He reached under the glass top and retrieved two crystal glasses.

"Vice President Chong, Sir." His eyes lifted as he heard Mahalia's voice introduce his visitor.

"Sam, you old son of a gun, how have you been? It's good to see you. I take it everything is well. Are you all settled in? Is there anything you need?" Grimm despised the way Chong's hair was slicked back, pasted to his head.

Sam Chong, immaculate in a tailor-made black suit and silk tie, walked slowly to the bar and climbed on one of the cheetah skin-covered stools. He stared into Grimm's eyes, expressionless, waiting for Grimm to get uncomfortable with the lack of response. Grimm turned his gaze away from him and Chong's lip curled in satisfaction.

"We have a problem," Chong said. "A problem that should have been dealt with long before I got here. Oh, and maybe you should be paying more attention. I've been settled here for at least six months."

Grimm needed to get control of the conversation. "Can I offer you a scotch, cognac…?"

Chong leaned forward, his forearms on the glass top and his eyes burning.

"Nothing. I want nothing but your absolute attention to what I'm about to say. I was sent here by The Coalition to fix the disorder that you have allowed to develop. Do not misunderstand me, Grimm. Your position is strictly one of convenience. It gives the people here someone to focus on and to vent their hatred at."

Grimm stood erect and glared back. "Who the hell do you think you are? You don't come in here and talk to me like that. I run the show here." He stormed to the front of his desk and reached over to slam the button on his intercom. "Mahalia, get in here."

The door burst open and Grimm growled at Chong, "Get the hell out of here."

Chong slid off the barstool and sauntered past Grimm until he was behind the desk. He dropped into the chair, leaned back, and placed his patent leather oxfords on the desk.

"You might want to call the Capitol before you get too far into the hole you're digging for yourself," he said. "Like I said, I was sent here to clean up your mess."

Grimm scowled and hesitated. His lips drew a tight line across his face as he turned to Mahalia.

"Mahalia. Get me corporate headquarters, please."

The side door of the garage groaned as the ancient hinges moved, one side grinding against the other. Nora Walsh stepped over the threshold into the makeshift meeting room in Charles Fleming's garage. Once her eyes adjusted to the interior light she could make him out at the far end of a homemade table.

"Hi, Charles," she called out as she took in the room. "Looks like I'm the first one here. OK to turn the light on?" She was still in her nurse's uniform as there had been no time to go home and get changed for this hastily called gathering. Although 60 years old, she still had the energy of a young woman, and only a slight sprinkling of silver shone through her brunette hair.

"Sure, turn 'em on. Coffee's in the pot," he said without raising his head as he continued stacking paper on the table. His plaid, buttoned shirt hung loosely on his frame, giving the appearance of being the wrong size. As usual, his long hair was unruly.

When he was satisfied that the documents were ready, he turned to Nora. His usual bright, inquisitive eyes were tired and his haggard, unkempt appearance showed the strain he was under. He crossed the floor to her and they embraced.

"I'm glad you're here," he said. "There's been so much going on. I just don't know what to do." He glanced down at the documents piled on the table.

"Well, tell me. Don't keep it to yourself," said Nora. She was concerned for her old friend.

"Let's wait for the others," he said as he pressed his lips together. "I don't think I have it in me to repeat this over and over."

The door burst open, startling them.

"Hi guys," came the cheerful chorus of voices as Danielle and Sherry Fraser arrived. Their marriage 20 years earlier had been protested by the supporters of the ultra-right faction that was in power at the time and they had been working against the regime ever since. They moved into the welcoming hugs from Nora and Charles.

"You gotta close the door behind you," said Danielle. "You never know who might be listening in."

"Oh, you're suspicious of everything," said Sherry.

"Sometimes you have to be, "Danielle retorted.

"Grab a coffee if you want, or some illicit H2O if that's your preference," smiled Charles.

The four of them sat around the table and began chatting. The innocuous discussion on the weather, their jobs and the neighbourhood quickly dissipated. Charles slid individual packets of paper from the piles on the table toward each of them.

"I don't know if you've noticed or not," he said, "but this new vice president they brought in from China to deal with peace and well-being makes everything we've faced so far look like a cakewalk. He's introduced some new regulations that are going to make life even more difficult."

"What the hell more can he do?" said Danielle. "It's already illegal to grow your own food and get your own water. It's their fault everything's in such a mess anyway."

"So, what's going on now?" asked Nora, her brow furrowed.

Charles shuffled through the stack of paper in front of him.

"Look on page 36, he said. "It's more on the enforcement end. Not enough people are complying with the corporate demand that all water and food be bought from The Coalition for Citizens' Benefit and their approved sources, so they had Parliament enact punishments that are right out of the Middle Ages."

Nora stood and began pacing the length of the table, holding her coffee in both hands. Her unfocused eyes faced straight ahead. She stopped at the head of the table and slowly turned to face those that were seated.

"Charles, don't exaggerate. What do you mean right out of the Middle Ages?" Although she had never voiced it, her biggest fear was that The Coalition would use violence to coerce the populace into accepting their demands.

"Jail time for a first offence of collecting water. Further offences could result in corporal punishment."

"How can they do that? Where did they get the right?" asked Sherry.

"They were given the authority to make the rules from an international tribunal a couple of years ago and then Parliament added them to the Criminal Code," said Charles. "What we have to do now is persuade people to join us to put an end to it all. What you have in front of you are copies of the new orders and penalties. Maybe if we petition President Grimm he'll ease off on some of this."

"I agree," Nora said, "surely he has some control over this vice president."

"There's a problem with that plan," said a voice from the doorway. Charles's 19-year-old son, Brad, leaned back against the door jamb, his hands thrust into his pockets. "There's another regulation that's in force that has not been made public yet. You can learn a lot through a little computer hacking."

Charles eyes shone proudly as he looked at his tall, dark-skinned son. Brad had grown into a young man of substance and value. His looks and mannerisms brought memories of his mother, Sharon, causing a mist to appear over Charles' face. The beautiful Tlingit woman had died under mysterious circumstances after the first fracking incident north of Whitehorse.

"So, what else have you found out?" asked Charles.

"It's an offence to conspire against The Coalition." Brad moved over to the table.

"It has been since they took over, hasn't it?" asked Danielle.

"Yes, but now it's considered treason," said Brad as he sat down.

"Treason? How can it be treason?" Charles asked. "Is this the result of what started with a government back around 2011 who insisted that anyone who disagreed with them or questioned them was a radical—an anti-Canadian? God help us. Now look what it's evolved into."

The silence in the room was deafening.

Sherry connected with the eyes of each of the others and asked softly, "I wonder what Galen's going to have to say. I'm sure he won't be happy."

Chapter 3

Paddy gasped for breath as he stumbled through the underbrush at the top of the hill. His wounded shoulder screamed in agony and his aching legs were failing him. He checked Keira and saw that her eyes were closed. Aaron and Gwen caught up to him as he sank to the ground.

"Let me have her," Gwen said.

He didn't have the energy to resist. Gwen rolled Keira forward toward her and grasped her close to her chest as Paddy fell backward and lay still except for his deep breaths.

"Is she going to be okay, Mom?" asked Aaron.

"She'll be fine, Honey. We're going to take her to see the doctor and she'll be fine."

Gwen moved closer to Paddy. "We've been going for a long time. When will we get to the car?" she whispered.

Paddy rolled to his side and pushed himself into a sitting position. His head turned from one side to the other as he searched the bush around them. He hung his head.

"I'm not sure," he replied. "I thought we would be there by now. If we could just find that stream."

Keira convulsed in Gwen's arms. Her eyes bulged as she spewed vomit on the ground. Gwen knew they had to keep moving. She was holding Keira with one arm and trying to help Paddy stand when she saw a wolf through the trees.

"Get up!" she screamed at Paddy. "Aaron, get over here!" She thrust Keira into Paddy's arms and grabbed a piece of wood she found lying on the ground. She raised it over her shoulder as she peered into the brush, looking for the beast.

"You won't be needing that, ma'am," a gentle voice announced. She spun around holding the length of log above her head and snarled into the face of the man in front of her.

"It's okay, ma'am, you can put that down now. Bob's as gentle a dog as was ever born, especially with kids. Now, put down that stick and tell me what's going on here," Landon's soothing voice continued. She calmed as his soft eyes and greying pony-tail disarmed her.

She stared at him momentarily, and then dropped to the ground as her shoulders slumped in surrender.

"She got sick, I don't know why. Paddy's hurt. We are lost. I don't know what to do."

"It's okay, ma'am," said Landon as he touched her arm, "let's have a look at what's going on."

Landon stepped past her and rubbed his hand on the top of Aaron's head as he made his way over to Paddy and Keira. He noticed the dried blood around the hole torn in the front of Paddy's right shoulder as he gently lifted Keira from Paddy's arms, felt her forehead and softly lifted each eyelid. What he saw disturbed him.

"We need to get them both to the hospital as quickly as possible," Landon said. "I don't know how you got this far back in the bush but I need to know if you have a car or if we need to go back to my place to get one."

"Our SUV is at the beginning of the trail leading from Fish Lake," said Paddy. "It can't be too far from here."

Landon pulled a breath between closed teeth. "You've been travelling in the wrong direction. We need to go straight east until we hit the trail and then due south. Let me carry the girl. Bob will lead us there. Please, we have no time to waste."

It took an hour and a half before they crossed the creek where it flowed over the path. Two hours beyond that, Gwen handed her daughter to the nurse in Emergency.

"Is she going to be okay? We got her here as quickly as we could." Gwen's tears streamed through the dirt on her face. "Tell me she's going to be okay."

"We'll do everything possible for her," said the nurse as she turned and hurried into the treatment area, shouting to the receptionist to get the doctor on call to stop everything he was doing and get to Emergency immediately.

She stopped and glanced back at Gwen and asked, "What's her name?"

"Keira," sobbed Gwen.

The nurse rushed away, talking constantly to the child. "Stay with me, Keira. I'm here for you. Listen to me, Keira, I need you to stay with me. Keira, my name is Nora. Stay with me..." They disappeared from view behind the curtains as Gwen slumped into a chair in the Emergency waiting area. A hospital social worker asked to watch over Aaron, and Gwen nodded slowly.

Meanwhile, Paddy had been sedated and treated for the puncture wound to his shoulder and was then admitted for observation because of its quickly advancing infection. It appeared to be under control, but they were concerned because of the speed of his decline.

Gwen sat alone and waited...and prayed.

Several hours passed before Nora returned to the waiting room, hesitating at the door. She took a deep breath, and walked through. Gwen stood and rushed toward her.

"How is she? Is my baby going to be all right? What is—" Gwen froze as she caught the answer in the nurse's eyes.

Nora gently guided her into a large chair and knelt beside her.

Gwen studied Nora's face. "No, no!" she sobbed.

"I'm so sorry. The doctor said nothing could be done," she said, looking into Gwen's eyes as they filled with tears.

Gwen stared at Nora silently for a moment, and then began a soft moan that grew quickly into a momentous wail. She stood, blinded by the pain. Nora drew her close and wrapped her arms around her. The two women stayed enveloped in each other for a number of minutes. Then, abruptly, Gwen drew away.

"What was it?" she demanded, her eyes blazing. "What was wrong with her? How can a perfectly healthy child suddenly become so sick...and then...how?"

"Let's go to Paddy's room," suggested Nora. "We'll talk there. I think the two of you need each other right now."

Gwen wasn't sure she wanted to see Paddy at that moment. She was still undecided about why they had been in the woods in the first place and whose fault it was that it had all happened. At the same time she was worried about Paddy's injury and why it had become horribly inflamed so quickly—and what was happening with Aaron through all this? She was frightened and angry, and felt so alone.

Nora led her down the flat beige corridor to the ward where Paddy was recuperating. They stopped at room 212.

"Take a few breaths," Nora suggested. "You need to breathe." Gwen gasped some air, then straightened, gave her head a shake and pushed through the door.

Gwen saw the stain on Paddy's cheeks where his tears had flowed. His blood-shot eyes filled again as he met her gaze. The combined effect of the infection and the medications made it impossible for him to move or to even say much, but she could see he was still in pain. His eyelids appeared heavy as he fought to keep them open.

"I'm so sorry," he muttered. "Is she OK?"

Gwen couldn't respond. Nora moved to the head of the bed and placed her hand on Paddy's arm.

"I'm sorry, Mr. Doyle."

Paddy's eyes closed and his body wracked with sobs as he attempted to catch his breath. Gwen leaned over and held him. Eventually he opened his eyes and connected with the two women, his pillow soaked.

"What about Aaron?" he asked. "Where is he? Does he know?"

"He's with a hospital social worker," Nora said. "He doesn't know yet. We'll tell him later."

Gwen picked up a towel to dry Paddy's face, and then stopped and turned to Nora, her eyes questioning. "What happened? What can you tell us?"

"It was acute cyanide poisoning," Nora said. "There were other complications as well, from other toxins, but the cyanide was the worst."

Gwen and Paddy looked at each other, incredulous.

"Where would she get cyanide from?" asked Paddy. "It just doesn't make any sense."

Gwen stood bolt upright. "The creek—the creek that crossed the path. She drank from that creek..."

Monday morning found Stone and Kirsten in the Mining Recorder Office in Whitehorse. They were busy poring over the maps of the Whitehorse area when the phone rang. The man behind the counter grabbed the receiver and turned his back on them.

"We're waitin' for the new maps," he spoke, muffled into the phone. "The new mine west of here doesn't show up on any of the current ones." After a moment he said, "Well, get 'em here as soon as ya can."

Stone was interested. "Where is that mine?" he asked as he spread the map open.

The mining recorder stiffened. "What mine?" he asked, his eyes widening.

"You just said something about a mine that opened—west of Whitehorse," said Stone.

"Uh, you must have misunderstood somethin'," replied the mining recorder as he turned his back and began walking away, leaving Stone and Kirsten standing at the counter, perplexed.

"Come on," Stone prompted. "You can show us where that mine is located. I don't see one here. Is that because it is so new it isn't on the map yet?"

"I can't discuss it if it ain't on the map," the man said without turning around.

Kirsten moved to the end of the counter closer to where he sat. "Look, uh, sorry, what was your name again?"

The man glanced up from his computer screen, his brows furrowed. "Brian," he answered.

She leaned forward on the counter and smiled. "Well, Brian, my name is Kirsten Allerton. I'm a journalist doing some research on how the mining industry is getting along in Yukon and how much it is providing to the economy. Anything you tell me is confidential because I don't have to reveal my sources. So, you see, you're not really talking to the public, you're talking with a reporter. So everything is okay."

His eyes were fixed on his hands as they rested on his keyboard. He pressed his lips together, slowly shook his head, then stood and walked over to the counter.

"I really shouldn't do this. If word gets out I'll lose my job or worse. But it's drivin' me nuts the way they're gettin' away with destroyin' everything."

He focused directly into Kirsten's eyes. "You're sure nobody will know?"

"They'll never hear it from me."

His face softened and his shoulders dropped as he let out a large breath. "There's a mine, about 20 miles west of Whitehorse, as the crow flies…" he began.

Kirsten marvelled as Stone guided the little Prius around the curves on the Alaska Highway. She was impressed by the ease in which he handled the vehicle while scouring the roadsides for a sign of exit. *I wonder what the folks back home in Toronto would think*, she wondered as she admired his strong profile. She liked the way his hair moved as he turned his head from the side and back to watch the mirrors and the road. The muscles in his forearm rippled as he manoeuvred the steering wheel.

"Kirsten. Kirsten? Hey, Kirsten!"

She startled in her seat, caught Stone's eyes and giggled. Then she turned and watched out the window as the scenery went by.

"I guess I was daydreaming." She peeked back at him and blushed. He didn't seem to notice.

They had been driving up and down the same stretch of highway west of Whitehorse for close to four hours. Explorations up several side roads had proved fruitless, either ending at somebody's property or stopped at a dead-end. They were tired, hungry and frustrated.

"I'm starved," said Stone. "Let's go back to town and get something to eat. Then we'll figure out what to do."

There was nagging in the back of his mind but he couldn't quite figure out what it was—something that the man in the Mining Recorder Office had said.

They returned to the restaurant where Kirsten had been the day they met, and ordered paninis with strong coffee and then sat side-by-side on the bench behind the table in Kirsten's favourite spot in the corner facing Main Street.

"I don't understand why we're not finding a road to the mine," Kirsten said, leaning back in the seat. "He said it was 20 miles west."

Stone turned to her. "I know. It doesn't make any sense. A roadway to a mine should be well marked or at least easy to find. The imprint from the equipment alone should give it away." He loved the way the sunlight from the window created shimmering highlights in her hair.

They sat in silence eating their meal, each lost in their own thoughts. Absentmindedly, Kirsten turned the salt shaker. With each turn the glass bottom scraped on the wood table. Stone placed his hand over hers to silence the movement. The touch was electric. Kirsten was surprised. She sat staring straight ahead out onto Main Street, not daring to look in his direction. She hadn't felt this way in a long time.

"You okay?" he asked.

28

"Yeah, I guess so. It just bothers me that we're not making any headway on this. I'm curious why that guy, Brian, was so afraid to talk about mines. That's his job, to register and provide information on mines. Then when he finally does give us some information it doesn't seem to be correct. And what the hell does 'as the crow flies' mean?"

"Why do you ask?" said Stone.

"That's what Brian said," returned Kirsten. "Twenty miles as the crow flies."

Stone's eyebrows raised and his eyes opened as his face broke into a wide grin.

"That's it! That's what I missed. Grab your coffee and your sandwich and let's go."

"That's what? What on earth are you talking about?"

"As the crow flies means a straight line," said Stone as he snatched his things. "We've been following roads and highways looking for a way to get to a mine that might be right in our backyard. Shit, I wonder what else I missed hearing him say."

"I thought you were listening to it all," Kirsten said as she hurriedly grabbed at the remaining food. "I was just focusing on getting him to talk. He said something about private property. Yeah. That was it, private property. Oh, I remember, he said the entrance to the mine was private property. No, that wasn't it. The entrance to the mine was on private property."

"So it could be that one of the properties we came across this morning actually hides the entrance road to a mine?" Stone asked incredulously. "Why would they do that?"

He stepped toward her as she stood and wrapped his arms around her. "Let me help you grab your stuff, Kirsten. I have an idea that may get us some answers. Let's go."

She smiled as her cheeks reddened from his embrace. "I gather that this could take a while. I'm going to go pee first."

Stone laughed out loud. "Maybe I should too."

Chapter 4

Bob's eyes closed as his 35 kg body curled up on the front seat of the old Chevy half-ton. Landon's fingers absently scratched the sweet spot between the dog's ears, barely paying enough attention to the road to keep them between the ditches on the gravel road toward Fish Lake. His vision blurred as he thought of the little girl he helped take to the hospital. Was it only a week ago? Her death brought back so many memories.

His wife, Wenda, had died in the summer of 2021. Her symptoms were almost identical to those of little Keira's. He still felt the helplessness of holding Wenda's hand as the abdominal pain doubled her over with convulsions. The vomiting, the diarrhea, dehydration; it was all just too much to think of. There were others, many others, but various departments from The Coalition for Citizens' Benefit insisted that everything was under control. Landon wasn't so sure. He only wanted to stay away from everyone and everything, hiding like a hermit in his cabin. But the thought of what had happened to Wenda and Keira spurred him on.

As he reached the northern tip of the lake, passing the parking lot and starting up the single lane road following the shore, a flash of white at the water's edge caught his eye. The tires dug into the sand as he hit the brakes. He stepped out of the truck, waiting long enough for Bob to bound off the seat and onto the sandy, rock-strewn beach. The dog immediately stopped with his head held high and ears pointed forward. He then lowered his nose to the ground and began pacing back and forth trying to connect with the source of the strange scent he had detected.

Landon went directly to the shore, searching for whatever it was that had caught his attention. Both of them caught sight of it at the same time. It was a Glaucous Gull, or rather, something that used to be a gull. He had never seen a dead gull before. *Seems damn strange*, he thought, *but I really need to keep going.*

He shepherded the old truck up the dirt trail that followed the shoreline and continued in a southerly direction. An hour later he was examining the deep ruts that had been left in the dirt by the Doyles' Sportage as it tore away from its parking spot a few days before. He glanced up at the footpath leading into the woods and called Bob to his side.

"Well, old fella, it looks like we got some things to learn," he said as he knelt to ruffle the dog's ears. "I have no idea what we're looking for but I sure hope I recognize it when we see it."

Bob moved back and forth wagging his tail, alternating glances between Landon and the forest path. Landon shouldered a backpack with food and water, strapped on his Magnum and grabbed the Winchester from behind the seat. He reached into the cargo box, took out a walking stick, glanced down one more time at the ruts and walked around the back bumper, and then struck off up the trail.

I wonder who that belongs to, he thought as he caught sight of a bright orange Toyota Prius that had been backed into a small opening between the trees. *Probably just some hikers. I hope they have a better day than the Doyles did.*

Kirsten sat on a fallen log and watched as the water lapped at the shore. Stone, up to his knees in the lake, cautiously stepped back and forth moving a piece of branch in front of him. He was trying to find something in the water that may have caused the dead lake trout that were washed up on the sand, their remains rotting in the sunlight. The body of one gull lay under a tree. The ravens overhead were squawking and calling constantly.

"Is this something unusual?" Kirsten asked.

"It's certainly nothing I've ever seen before," said Stone. "It's very strange. Fish don't normally die all in one spot, unless it's salmon spawning, and I have never seen a dead gull. Something that's even more unusual is that the ravens haven't touched these fish. They're staying well away from them and seem to be upset either with our being here or, maybe, with the fact that these fish are dead and something is wrong. Ravens have a way of knowing when there is danger."

After 20 minutes of searching through the water, Stone decided he wasn't going to find anything. He walked up on the shore and snatched a towel from his backpack and then dried off his legs and feet and pulled his socks and hiking boots back on before moving over and sitting beside Kirsten. She snuggled into his side and laid her head on his shoulder as he put his arm around her.

"What do you think we're getting into?" she asked as she turned her face up to him.

"Not really sure. But I do know we have to keep trying to find out what caused this. If it's starting to get to be too much for you, let me know and I'll take you back to town. I don't want you feeling uncomfortable." Stone drew her closer.

"We started this together so we'll keep going together," Kirsten smiled. "Besides, there may be a great story to be found here." She turned her gaze over the water. "So, what's next?"

Stone's eyes followed upstream of the creek that was emptying into the lake. "I guess we follow that stream," he said as he stood and reached down to help Kirsten stand.

The two of them shouldered their gear and started walking through the forest beside the creek, their eyes seeking any information that may lie in wait.

Landon had reached the stream that Gwen said Keira drank from. It seemed innocuous enough, flowing over its bed, appearing clear and clean. His attention turned to Bob who had, without hesitation, turned and started moving upstream with his head down, tracking a scent. Landon decided that was as good a direction as any at that point so moved along behind the dog checking the firmness of the creek bank with a walking stick. The sounds of the forest and the late morning sunlight filtering through the trees were calming as he trudged up the trail.

After an hour or so, they stopped to eat and drink. Bob jumped to his feet, agitated. A slight whine escaped him as his body tensed and his full attention was directed downstream. Landon gathered everything, leaving no trace of having been there and then moved into a spot behind the trees holding the Winchester in readiness, every muscle tense.

Landon was quiet and sharply attentive as he scrutinized the creek banks, watching for any sign of movement. Bob sat motionless beside him. There was flicker of colour and movement, and then a young man and woman appeared through the brush as they walked alongside the creek. *Must be those hikers*, Landon thought as he watched them stop at the spot where he and Bob had been moments before. The young man stopped, checked all around, and called out.

"Hello? Hello? I know you're here. Hello? Come on out," said Stone.

Kirsten followed directly behind Stone, wondering what he was talking about as he turned in all directions.

A small movement caught Stone's attention. "Ah, there you are," he said as his eyes bore over his right shoulder.

He watched as Landon stepped out from behind the trees, Bob by his side.

"Hi. I didn't mean to scare you," Landon said as he brushed some leaf remnants from his arm. "I thought Bob here had smelled himself a bear or something."

Stone frowned slightly as he studied the well-armed man in front of him, at the same time keeping himself between the stranger and Kirsten. "You with the government? You seem to be equipped for almost anything."

"Hell no," grinned Landon. "More interestingly though, how did you know I was here? I thought I had picked everything up."

Stone's eyebrows rose. "Maybe, but the smell of a beef sandwich with onion tends to linger in the air for a while."

Landon laughed out loud. "The name's Landon. And you?"

Stone smiled as he relaxed his stance. "They call me Stone, and this is Kirsten. So, are you just out for a little stroll in the woods?"

"Nice to meet you—and you too, Kirsten," he said as he moved his head to get a look at her behind Stone. Kirsten leaned over to the side so she could see Landon and then smiled.

"Not really," he continued. "I'm curious about this creek; curious about where it starts and where it flows before it gets here. So, to satisfy my curiosity I thought I'd take a walk and see where it leads me."

Stone observed Landon for a moment before deciding to accept what he said. "Have you noticed something different about this creek from any other you've seen?" he asked as he surveyed the rippling water.

Kirsten furrowed her brow and stepped out from behind Stone. She knelt beside the creek, examining it. Landon considered the stream as well. He thought there was something odd about it but he just couldn't quite put his finger on it. He wanted to know what Stone was thinking.

"Other than the fact that it runs across the path further down, I'm not really sure what it is that seems different," said Landon.

Stone knelt beside the creek and motioned for Kirsten and Landon to come beside him.

"Look through the water into the bed of the creek. Do you see anything unusual?"

"I'm afraid this city girl wouldn't know what to look for," said Kirsten as she tickled her fingers into the coolness.

Stone waited patiently while Landon inspected the water. His eyes moved up and down its length, watching the current go by. He frowned deeply as he contemplated the creek banks, bed and the water as it bubbled over a couple of rocks. Bob sidled over to him and put his front feet into the water, causing a cloud of mud to flow past the three of them. As Bob's muzzle neared the stream and his tongue shot out to catch the cool liquid, Landon shouted, "No!"

Bob jumped out of the water and ran about 5 metres then stopped and turned back questioningly at Landon.

"Sorry, old boy," said Landon as he motioned Bob back to him. "I'll give you a drink from a clean water supply."

He turned back to Stone and Kirsten. "Look, just so you know, I'm really concerned about the safety of this water. Something tells me you're wondering about it as well."

"I'm not sure what it is you're thinking, Landon, but maybe it's something we can work on together," said Stone.

"Well, I'll be damned," said Landon. "It's starting to look like we're on the same page. If you're trying to find out what's wrong with this water and what's causing it, then yep, we just might be able to work together."

Kirsten caught Stone's eye. "Well, what is it that you saw? What makes this creek different?" she asked.

Stone moved toward the water's edge and put his hand into the flow and touched the bottom, causing silt to rise.

"A long-established creek in this area would have a bed consisting only of stones and rocks. There would be no fine sand left. See the pieces of wood and leaves still stuck at the bottom? That tells me this stream hasn't been here very long. The question is what caused it to start flowing here and where did it come from?"

A motion caught their eyes and they turned to see Bob already headed up-stream, due north. Landon placed his walking stick firmly into the bank of the stream and with a glance back at his two new friends, began following. Kirsten and Stone locked eyes and, as if the answer came to both congruently, nodded and took the first steps toward the source of the water.

Main Street in Whitehorse was almost deserted when Paddy brought the old Kia to a stop in front of The People's Pub. He shut the engine off and sat, listening to the quiet. There was a time when Friday nights in the middle of downtown bustled with people in coffee shops while others scuttled to and fro. His parents had told him about a time when the stores on Main would stay open until 9:00 p.m. and would be filled with shoppers until closing.

But all that was before *The Agreement*, he thought. *Now, the stores are all closed by six, even the coffee shops are empty by seven. Oh, well, there's always the pub.*

He went to the pub to forget; if only he could forget...

He slid through the door and waited for his eyes to adjust to the dim lighting. A young woman with an overly full head of blond locks was crooning an ancient country song, backed up by a three piece band of nondescript musicians. Round tables were strewn about the room with no particular organization in mind, each with four chairs leaning into it. Several tables had people, mostly men, leaning forward toward the centre, clutching their beer glasses and, no doubt, carrying on discussions of worldly import.

Paddy sat at a table at the back of the pub where he could nurse his drinks in privacy and not be bothered by anyone. He slipped off his jacket and leaned back on the chair.

"What'll it be?"

He turned his eyes up to see the girl; short, fire-red hair, multiple piercings in her left ear and the beginnings of a set of tattoos on her forearms that were covered by the sleeves of her black, translucent blouse. A short black skirt over mesh stockings and a heavy set of black work boots finished the look.

"Hi. Bring me a pitcher, please."

"Anything to eat?" she asked.

"No, thanks." He noticed her tongue stud.

There was only a couple of men he recognized in the bar that night; the mechanic that fixed the Sportage when it broke down a year or so earlier and another, a smaller man with thick glasses who he had gotten to know over chats in this very establishment. Paddy had enjoyed those discussions and liked the way the man presented himself.

Ron, thought Paddy as his gaze remained fixed on the man with the glasses. *Yeah, that was his name. Nice guy.*

His contemplations were interrupted by the appearance of a pair of blue jeans at the edge of his table. He looked up to see Billy Thorsen, one of the local bar-flies.

"This seat taken? Mind if I join you?" Billy said without waiting for an answer as he sat opposite Paddy.

Paddy forced a smile. "Doesn't look like I have much of a choice. Haven't seen you for a while."

"I've been away. Well, sittin' in jail if you really need to know. I made the mistake of not obeyin' an order from one of those fuckin' militia assholes quick enough. Charged me with obstructin' justice or somethin' like that. Three months I got. I still don't know why fer sure."

The pitcher of beer arrived and was set on the table with a glass in front of Paddy. Billy caught Paddy's eyes, questioning.

"Bring another glass, please," said Paddy.

"Good to see you again, Marsha," Billy said to the waitress.

"I'm going by Star now," she retorted. "I'll bring you a glass."

Billy watched the movement of Star's behind as she stepped away from the table and sashayed across the room. When she was out of sight he turned back to Paddy.

"Yeah, those guys are real assholes," Billy said. "Shit, we thought it was bad when we had the damn RCMP but these guys are really somethin' else. So what's been goin' on with you?"

Paddy stared into his beer and remained silent. He didn't have the strength to start talking about his loss and the pain his family had been in since Keira's death—not to the likes of Billy. Gwen was angry and sullen most of the time; Aaron was acting out with behaviours that were, previously, unlike him. Paddy had withdrawn from everything. He just couldn't face it.

"Just life," he mumbled.

The door burst open as three men in black trench coats walked into the pub. Two of them, well over 2 metres tall and appearing quite muscular, stood on either side of a much smaller man, bald and slight in stature but whose expression and eyes indicated that he was spoiling for trouble. Each step the small man took was mirrored by the other two. Josef Poste had recently been assigned as the Director of Militia Activities in Whitehorse. It was his job to ensure that peace was maintained and that the laws of The Coalition for Citizens' Benefit were followed and he

40

brought his muscle everywhere with him to assure enforcement.

Poste wore a sneer as he walked through the bar, stopping at each table to glare at its occupants. As he made the rounds he came to the table where Paddy and Billy were seated. He leaned over, placing one hand on the table, and put his face close to Paddy's, his brows folded inward.

"Do I know you?" he asked.

"I don't think so, Sir. We haven't had the pleasure of meeting before."

"Seems to me I know you from somewhere..."

Without shifting his body position he turned his head toward Billy. "You I know. How was your little, um, holiday, shall we say. I trust the staff at the hotel treated you well." He stared in Billy's face, laughing. Billy kept his eyes averted and said nothing.

Poste stood, turned and continued walking between the tables, his two goons marching in step. He bypassed a couple of groups of men before stopping at the table where Ron Jerome sat alone.

"And what's your story?"

"Excuse me?" asked Ron.

"Gimme some ID," Poste demanded.

"Have I done something wrong? I'm just sitting here having a beer. What have I done wrong?"

"I'll ask the questions. Are you saying you don't have any ID?"

Ron reached into the inside lapel pocket of his sports coat to retrieve his wallet. As he did so Poste yelled, "Keep your hands where I can see them!" The two men with him grasped the night sticks inside their long coats.

"But you said you wanted ID."

"Are you arguing with me? Think you're a big man?"

Poste reached forward and grabbed the glasses off of Ron's face. "Blind as a bat without these, aren't you? What would you do if you didn't have them?"

"Please, Sir, let me have my glasses back. I can't see without them. Just tell me what you want and I'll make sure you get it. My ID is in my coat pocket, here," Ron said as he reached again toward the inside pocket.

Poste reacted instantly by backhanding him across the face. The two uniformed men with him grabbed Ron's arms and pulled them behind the chair, pinning him in place helplessly. Poste unceremoniously dropped the eyeglasses on the floor. The cracking of glass and the scrape of metal into the wood could be heard as he ground his heel on them.

"Take him outside. He needs to learn to obey us when we talk to him; anything else is obstructing justice." Poste scoured the faces in the room to see if anyone dared defy him.

Paddy stood at his table, his body trembling in anger. He watched as they dragged Ron across the floor and out the door. He wanted, desperately, to go to Ron's rescue, but the fear of reprisal kept him rooted in place. He slumped back into his chair and let his gaze drop to the floor.

Later, they would learn that Ron Jerome did not have to serve time for obstruction of justice. He died in a back alley, alone. The official release stated that he was a victim of a robbery.

Chapter 5

Dust shrouded the road behind the Subaru station wagon as Nora made her way eastward on Burma Road toward the Fleming home overlooking the Yukon River. Galen Hamel sat in the passenger seat with the seatbelt locked tightly around him, his head nodded forward. She smiled, realizing that he was sound asleep. At 85, he sometimes found it difficult to stay awake for lengthy periods, particularly while in a vehicle.

She rounded a left curve and then followed along the river bank for about half a mile before she saw the sign in front of the acreage where Charles and his son Brad lived. The Fleming garage was the location of numerous clandestine meetings of a group of friends who wanted to put a stop to the environmental damage and control of people that came from The Coalition. Generally a peace-loving group, frustrations were mounting and anger was becoming more apparent as time went on. Its out of the way locale was safer than meeting in town.

As she pulled up the driveway toward the garage she could see that Danielle and Sherry had already arrived and were carrying on an animated conversation with Charles. The three of them were laughing, each trying to talk over the other as they watched her approach. The car came to a halt, kicking up some dust in the driveway. Galen coughed, sat up straight, and then smiled as he saw his friends. It had been a matter of weeks since he was feeling up to the 25 km journey to the Flemings. Today, however, he felt as healthy and as spry as ever.

Charles rounded the car to the passenger side and opened the door, overjoyed to see his old friend. He grasped Galen's hand, shaking it fervently as he helped him out of the vehicle.

"It's so good to see you. How have you been doing? It's been far too long," said Charles.

"Well, I had a flu for a while and then was just feeling tired most days. I seem to be doing well now. Good thing too. We have much to talk about. Another one of us has been picked off, although we're not sure if it was coincidence or intentional."

"Oh my God. Who was it?"

"I'll let Nora fill everybody in on that once we get settled inside," said Galen. "She has far more information on it than I do."

Danielle and Sherry ran up to join them, taking turns hugging Galen. Sherry had tears in her eyes. "I was so afraid I'd never see you again," she said.

Galen held her face in his hands and smiled at her. "You can't get rid of me that easily. There is still far too much to do. It does my heart good to see you all here," he said as he caught the attention of the others.

He scanned the open yard and was somewhat dismayed to see that there were only five of them present. He had hoped by this time that the numbers in their movement would have swelled dramatically, but it seemed more difficult to get people involved than he'd initially thought. He was pleased, however, with the loyalty and dedication of this small group. Then he remembered the younger Fleming.

He sought Charles out. "So what is young Brad doing with himself these days, Charles?"

"He got himself a job in the Communications and IT sector with the government so now he's another one of those public servants."

Galen frowned at Charles, leaving the question unasked. They stood looking at each other for what seemed like hours, but in reality was only a few seconds.

"It's all good, Galen. He hasn't deserted us. Having him there is quite useful. Trust me, he hasn't forgotten what happened to his mother, and still levels the blame directly at The Coalition and anyone who supports them."

"I wouldn't expect anything different from that young man. However, I was just thinking that it's a pretty dangerous place that he's in. I trust he's being very careful."

"I wouldn't have it any other way," said Charles as he walked toward the garage alongside Galen. The others followed with the three women catching up on news they had missed since they were last together.

As they stepped through the side door of the garage a large fibreglass container resting in the far corner caught Galen's attention.

"That looks like a water container. Isn't your well keeping up? That must wreak havoc on your garden."

"Interesting you should ask that," said Charles. "About a month ago the Department of Health and Social Services came out and informed me that we could no longer draw water from our well—something about public health and safety and the possibility of noxious chemicals polluting the water. They said that no one can have a well any longer and that we have to have water delivery from an approved source. They said it's a matter of public safety.

"And then they tore up my garden saying it isn't allowed any longer. My entire life has been devoted to growing my own food and now I'm not allowed to. This has to come to an end."

The three women waved to Galen and Charles from across the room, inviting them to come to the table.

Charles placed his hand on the top of the water tank.

"They came a week later and capped my well off so I can't get anything out of it. Ironically enough, they still want me to continue paying back the loan they gave on our taxes to drill the well though."

Danielle went to the coffee pot, poured several cups and returned to the table. She set a cup in front of each of them.

Charles leaned forward on the table. "So, where do we start this?"

Nora shifted in her chair. "I'd like to know more about what has taken place to bring us to this sorry state of affairs," she asked. "How did Canada become so focused on everything but the environment and the welfare of people?"

Danielle reached over and took Sherry's hand, their eyes locked together. She turned to the others. "We're afraid because of how many people who have ended up sick, or worse. The way the militia is treating people seems to be getting harsher—more abusive, it seems."

Galen surveyed the group around the table and pursed his lips. He peered over the top of his glasses at his friends.

"I can tell you a bit of what I've seen, but know ahead of time that my opinions are skewed by the fact that I've been around so long. Eighty-five years give a man some serious changes to deal with and more than a few disappointments and frustrations. That being said, if you want, I can share what I know…and what I believe."

Nora smiled at him. "That would be great, Galen. I'd like to hear something as straightforward as possible, some information with no hidden agenda."

They watched as Galen adjusted himself in his chair and sat back to catch each of their eyes individually.

"Well, it all began in a small town in central B.C. way back in 1951," he began. Then his face broke into a broad grin and his eyes twinkled. "Lighten up, folks. I know we're facing desperate times but you have to make the effort to live in the moment, and at this moment we are safe and among friends. There will be time enough for strife, struggle and hard feelings, but for now we can relax.

"It's true that I was born into a simpler time," he continued, "But it was also a time where change was desperately needed. Women and minorities had no rights, or very few, and all efforts toward change faced conflict with the authorities. The unwillingness of those in power to alter the status quo or give up some of their dominance is the one thing that remains the same. It took strong organization by labour and community groups to effect change.

"I think it's important to recognize that not everyone who came into power throughout the years could be considered to be bad or evil, as many people would paint them. Those who governed for the first dozen years after the turn-of-the-century were subject to some kind of misguided or misdirected paternalistic attitude that they knew what was best for everybody and as a result, they ignored everybody else while they went on about making the world a better place, at least as they saw it. Unfortunately, although they thought they were worldly and sophisticated, it turned out that in the world marketplace they were nothing more than neophytes and had no real understanding or knowledge of what was going on. It wasn't until a couple years after *The Agreement* when the lawsuits began and the judgements against the

Government of Canada started to bankrupt the country that they realized their mistake. Signing *The Agreement* was the first step in opening the floodgates as it set a precedent for many others to follow."

Sherry leaned forward in her seat and examined Galen's face. "I've never fully understood what *The Agreement* was really about. How could one simple agreement make such a huge change?"

Galen turned to her, his gnarled hands surrounding his cup, relishing the warmth on his joints. "The intent was to give a boost to the economy, to bring in money from other countries in order to extract minerals and other resources. The network of good old boys firmly believed that it would benefit Canadians. Unfortunately, they got out played by the large corporations and the governments that backed them."

"Why didn't people stop them?" Sherry frowned. "There must have been somebody around that saw it was going to be a problem."

"Secrets," Galen replied. "You see, secrecy in government began long before this century. By 2015, the general public was completely unaware of what was going on within the hallowed halls of those who governed them or by the bureaucrats that completed the work. By that time everything had become completely hidden, veiled within a culture of secrecy and deceit. Remember, the elected officials were people who believed they knew what was best for everybody else. In Yukon, we were misinformed by statisticians as well as political pundits. Statistics can be molded to say anything you would like them to say. So the veracity of the information provided, I believe, was questionable. I expect it was the same federally."

Danielle sat back scratching her head. "Galen, did you say that part of *The Agreement* allowed foreign companies to sue the Canadian government?"

Sherry was confused. "I don't understand. If *The Agreement* was a federal thing, why did it have such an impact in Yukon?"

"That is absolutely correct, Danielle," said Galen. "However, *The Agreement* allowed that they could sue if regulations were put in place by any level of government that hindered the company's ability to make money. And, Charles, that is a big part of the reason why Yukon felt the brunt of *The Agreement*. The companies that came in and bought the mining and gas and oil interests, with the blessing and encouragement of the government, I might add, were then in a position to write their own tickets. Governments were loath to force them to adhere to existing regulations for fear of a lawsuit.

"You see, elections became very expensive. They were no longer about who would represent the people the best. They became simple mudslinging matches with participants being loyal only to their parties. Parties fell prey to the demands of large corporations in order to receive funding from them. As it turned out, a number of these corporations were not even from Canada. Once elected, the ruling party were mere puppets for business interests. When The Coalition took over they kept the various levels of governments such as municipal, provincial, and federal intact in order to have someone to collect the taxes as well as someone who would be the party being sued if regulations were passed that interfered with profits of the corporations. That way, the government could be blamed rather than The Coalition. They don't even bother hiding the fact anymore. There is no longer any pretence."

"That still doesn't explain why people stood by and allowed it to happen," said Charles.

"Perhaps a quote from Martin Luther King Jr. explains the apparent apathy in so many Canadians," said Galen. "He is credited with saying 'There is an almost universal quest for easy answers and half-baked solutions. Nothing pains some people more than having to think.'"

"I'm really not sure, but even today when you talk to people, they still are willing to accept everything they're told by those in power, even as climate change continues to affect the environment and our water is fouled. Winters are warming up, summers are getting colder and the amount of rainfall in Yukon has been increasing exponentially, adding to the problem of water pollution. I believe this is a continuation of the downturn in the North American empire as we have known it. There is so much more, but we can't spend all our time dwelling on the past when there is much to do now."

Charles's puzzled expression attested to his curiosity. "If you believe that, why do you bother fighting against it?"

Galen grinned. "Because I really don't know what God's plan is. My job is to do the best that I can and be the best person I can be for today. But, I do have to stand up for what I believe is right."

Charles offered everyone another coffee, and then turned to Nora. "Galen said you had some information about someone who was killed?"

"Ron Jerome. They brought him in to the hospital so severely beaten that he was hardly recognizable. The police claim that he was a victim of robbery but rumour on the street says otherwise."

Once again silence permeated the room.

Galen placed both hands on the table in front of him and looked around at his friends.

"And at my age I don't have a lot of time left to help. So what do we want to do next?"

The five of them were quiet as they exchanged glances. It was Nora who finally broke the silence. "Maybe we could have a town hall meeting and find out what other people are thinking? We can't be the only ones who are concerned."

Gwen was incredulous, her eyes piercing as Paddy fidgeted and turned away from her demanding stare.

"You mean to tell me there were witnesses that saw all of that? And Ron was just sitting there? Nobody did a damn thing to help?"

Paddy glanced up then quickly lowered his view.

"What was anybody supposed to do?" he said. "They are the law around here now. Maybe he did something that they had to arrest him for. We don't know for sure if it was Poste and his goons that did it. After all, the official police statement is that Ron was robbed."

Gwen anchored her gaze directly on Paddy.

"God help us," she snapped at him. "We've been broken to the point where we won't support each other anymore. That needs to change, and if you don't have the guts to stand up for yourself, I'm sure there are some out there who will."

Paddy offered no response, his eyes remaining focused on his hands in his lap.

Gwen stood and grabbed her jacket. She slammed the door as she left, without looking back.

Chapter 6

They had followed the creek bed for about twelve kilometres when Bob's hackles raised and he was on full alert. Landon quietly called him back.

"What is it, boy?" he said as he scratched the dog behind his ears. Bob's tail wagged slowly but his attention was drawn upstream. "I think we better move carefully from here on in," Landon whispered to Kirsten and Stone.

They nodded their agreement. As if with some unstated understanding, all three stopped and slid their backpacks to the ground.

"We should decide how we want to proceed from here," said Stone. "I'm starting to get the feeling that there is a lot more to this than I initially thought."

Kirsten slid a recorder out of her backpack and dropped it into the breast pocket of her vest. Then, she sat on her bag on the bank of the stream and opened a granola bar and took out a bottle of water. Stone sat on the ground beside her while Landon moved another few metres away and peered into the bush toward the north. He returned to where the other two were sitting. The snack caught his eye.

"Good idea, Kirsten. It might be a while before we get to eat again. Judging from the way Bob is acting we must be getting close to something. God only knows what. It's already been a long day."

Kirsten was tingling with a combination of anticipation and fear as she finished her food. "Do you have any idea what we're going to find?" she asked Landon. "Are we really going to find anything?"

Landon pulled a bottle of water from his backpack and poured a small amount into his cupped hand for Bob. The dog lapped at it greedily.

"I really have no idea. I'm just following this on a hunch, although after learning what Stone pointed out, I'm even more curious. I'd like to know why this creek is running here when it obviously wasn't present a short time ago."

Stone took a long draw from his water bottle and then focused his gaze on the stainless steel cylinder.

"There's something we haven't mentioned to you yet," he began as his eyes flashed toward Landon. "At the spot where this creek empties into Fish Lake we found something quite interesting. For some reason, a number of fish were dead and washed up on shore. And, the ravens and other scavengers were leaving the corpses alone. It kind of leads me to believe that there's something dreadfully wrong with the water in this creek."

Landon's brow furrowed as he massaged his chin. "A little over a week ago a little girl died after drinking from this stream," he said. "The hospital said that cyanide was the main poison but there were other noxious substances in her system as well. My God, there's been too many problems with the water around here for the last few years. I want to know more about what's going on and I thought this creek would be a good place to start." He glanced upstream, and then back to his companions.

Stone patted Kirsten's knee and smiled. "If you're ready to go I guess we should keep moving." She gave him a quick kiss on the cheek and stood and slid her arms through the straps of her backpack, hoisting it to her shoulders.

Landon kept Bob close to his side as they moved further upstream. They had gone less than half a kilometre when a razor-wire topped chain-link fence blocked their path, running from west to east. It had private property signs posted every 10 metres. The forest on the other side of the fence was so dense they couldn't see more than a few metres into it. After a short discussion they decided to follow the fence rather than go over or under it. None of them had any tools to cut their way through.

They travelled east along the fence until reaching the corner that turned north. Another 500 meters further, a roadway came into sight that led to a gate that was manned by armed personnel. Landon motioned to the other two to hide behind the windrow on the south side of the road. The three of them huddled in the brush, close together. Bob lay nearby. The road and gateway were about 50 metres across so there was no way to get inside without being seen.

"What do we do now, guys?" whispered Kirsten.

"Not much we can do while it's still daylight," Landon suggested. "We'll wait until it starts to get dark and then figure out how we can get a better look. In the meantime, try to get some rest." Landon rolled onto his back and closed his eyes. The others watched, incredulous.

"How can anyone just go to sleep like that?" giggled Kirsten.

A couple hours later, Stone nudged Landon awake.

"It's dusk now," Stone said. "Going to be dark soon. I guess now's as good a time as any to come up with some kind of plan."

Landon sat up and stretched his arms above his head and let them fall to his lap. He crawled to the top of the windfall and studied the guards and the gate. There was open ground on both sides of the road, providing no cover to sneak past the two men.

He slid back down to where Stone and Kirsten waited.

Landon motioned for them to come close. "We need to create some kind of diversion," he said. "Something to take their attention away from the gate so at least one of us can get inside. I'm not quite sure how we can do that."

"How can I help?" asked Kirsten.

Stone touched her arm and smiled.

"This probably isn't something you should be getting into. I'd hate to see anything happen to you. No, we'll figure something out," he said, as he nodded toward Landon, and then turned back to Kirsten. "Maybe you can stay here and make sure the dog is quiet so he doesn't give us away."

Landon frowned at the reference to Bob. After all, it was Bob that brought them here in the first place. Kirsten shook her head and turned away from them.

Stone eased over to Landon. He leaned in close and spoke quietly.

"Maybe if one of us could get to the other side of the road without being seen and make some noise in the woods over there to get their attention, the other could climb over the fence on this side?"

Landon studied the fence. "I don't think anybody is climbing over this fence with that razor wire there. The only way in is through that gate."

"So, who's going to create a distraction and who's going in?" asked Stone.

"Not really sure," said Landon. "You're younger and quicker than me so you might be able to sneak in undetected but the problem is if you get caught you have much more to lose than I do. What do you think Kirsten?"

The two men turned to hear Kirsten's response, but she was nowhere to be seen. They checked back down the trail to see if she had started to return to the car, then up and down the windrow, but she was nowhere to be seen.

"Hello! Can you give a girl a hand?" They heard her voice from the other side of the mound of dirt.

Landon and Stone scrambled to the top of the windrow and watched as Kirsten walked toward the gate on the far side of the road. Her jacket was hanging in her hand and her breasts moved alluringly under her white tank top.

She smiled at the guard closest to her and flipped her hair back with her right hand.

"I could sure use a drink of water," she said. "Do you guys have any you can share?"

The man nearest to her smiled in return. He signalled to his co-worker to bring some water over for her. Kirsten moved over to the gate post and leaned back seductively on it, making sure she stayed on the opposite side of the two men from where Landon and Stone were waiting.

"Stay," Landon told Bob. He motioned to Stone and whispered, "Gutsy girl. It's now or never. Let's move."

"Damn, what if something happens to her?" retorted Stone. "We have to get her away from there."

Landon grabbed Stone by the shoulders.

"Listen, she put her ass on the line so we could get in there. So let's get in there and find out what's going on." He secured his handgun in its holster and then turned and laid his Winchester with the butt on the ground and the barrel leaning on his backpack.

They clambered up the windrow, rolling over the top and moved quickly toward the gate. They ran bent over to keep as low as possible, careful not to step on anything that would make a noise. Kirsten's eyes flickered toward them when they reached the gate, and then quickly back to the two guards.

"So, you boys have to stay here all night? That could be quite interesting." she purred.

"I hope she's only acting," whispered Stone as he stopped to look back.

Landon chuckled and then tapped Stone on the arm. He motioned to him to move forward and they ducked into the enclosure. They dove under the rusted hulk of an old Hummer that sat with one flat tire about 25 metres inside the fence. They lay quietly, listening to portions of the muffled conversation between Kirsten and the two guards.

"You're welcome to stay here with us," they heard one of them say.

Landon pointed to a building. "We'll head over there," he breathed. They scurried out from under the Hummer and dashed across the open yard until they were behind the wall of the workshop where they stopped to catch their breath and listen. The property was quiet and there appeared to be no one else on site except the two guards. But they knew they still had to be cautious.

There was a huge pile of soil behind the building. The two men clawed their way to the top and lay dumbstruck by what they saw on the other side. A very broad but relatively shallow open pit mine had been scoured out of the earth. The equipment rested silently where the operators had left them.

Stone frowned as he perused the scene. He rolled toward Landon.

"This is ridiculous, mining this close to a city," he said. His eyes returned to the huge depression in the soil. "I wonder why they're not running night shifts?"

"Probably to make sure that the sound of the operation doesn't attract visitors that they don't want to have to deal with," said Landon. He pointed across the void. "See over there? On the far side of the pit."

They walked down inside the pit and across the bottom to the area that Landon had pointed out. A roadway led out of the pit and down the small hill to a large pile of slag. It was obvious that this was a heap leaching operation. A creek ran from the north side of the property into a tailings pond and drained on the other side directly toward Fish Lake. The tailings pond was far too small for the size of the operation and would not be efficient enough to remove the cyanide, arsenic and other poisons that were used in the extraction of minerals.

Landon motioned to where the stream came onto the property.

"They've redirected a stream that used to flow somewhere else in order to get their water. That's why the creek we've been following appears to be so new. These bastards are poisoning the water system."

Stone nodded. "That'll mean the ecology has changed where it used to flow as well. No wonder they want to keep it quiet. Hell, I don't even see the company name on the gate or anywhere on the property."

"Okay, let's get out of here," Landon said.

They turned back and headed toward the gate where they had come in and cautiously made their way back to the Hummer. As they crawled under the old truck the voices at the gate were clearer and louder than before.

"Come on, baby, stick around. We'll show you a good time," a male voice demanded.

"No, I want to get going." Kirsten could be heard now, more insistent.

"Screw it," a second male voice countered, "she knows what she came for."

Stone dragged himself toward the front of the Hummer until he could see the gate. Kirsten was walking away from the two men when the larger of them leaped forward and grabbed her by the arm, spinning her around. Stone scrambled out from under the vehicle and ran toward them, his heart pounding.

Kirsten pulled her arm but was unable to get free of the man's grasp.

"Let go of me, you son of a bitch. I wouldn't go anywhere with you if you were the last man on earth!" She began kicking at him.

"Oooh, she's a feisty one," said the other guard. "I guess it's time she learnt a lesson."

A deep, throaty growl was heard from the top of the windrow and dirt and rocks flew as Bob launched himself at the big man's throat. The dog bit and snarled and slashed at the man until he was forced to release Kirsten's arm. She backed away but the only direction she could go was toward the compound. Baring his teeth, Bob stood between her and the big man, his hackles raised and a growl in his voice.

The second man ran to the guard shack and grabbed a rifle. Kirsten watched in horror as he brought the gun around to bear at the snarling Bob.

"Yeeeaaaaagh!" she shrieked as she ran and jumped on his back and wrapped her legs around his waist and clawed at his face with her hands. The assault rifle thudded to the gravel.

Stone joined the fray, stepping up to the larger of the two men. He swung a haymaker with his right fist and connected on the man's chin. The big man stumbled backward, tripped and fell. He collected himself quickly, then stood and faced Stone. The man slid a nightstick from his belt. His lip curled on one side as he stepped toward Stone. The other guard had managed to throw Kirsten to the ground. Bob ran to her and then stood between them, growling.

Unexpectedly, the roar of a powerful engine drowned out every other sound. The guards ran into the guard house, one grabbing the phone, the other pulling another rifle from under the desk. The Hummer came across the yard, spewing gravel and belching smoke out the tailpipe. Landon aimed it directly at the shack where the guards had run for cover. The building disintegrated beneath the powerful truck with an ear-splitting crash. Another roar of the engine backed it off the rubble. Landon skidded across the seat and pushed the passenger door open.

"Get in!" he yelled.

Kirsten clambered up the step into the Hummer and scrambled over the backrest into the back seat as Stone jumped into the front. She threw open the back door and Bob leaped in beside her. They tore away from the compound with the flat tire on the rear wheel flapping against the fender.

About 500 metres down the road, Landon pulled over to the left and ran the Hummer another 100 metres into the bush on the north side of the road where he ran it into a large tree.

"OK, everyone out. We need to go on foot from here. We'll cross the road to the south side and head back the way we came."

Kirsten leaned over the seat. "What about the stuff we left back near the compound?" she asked.

"That's part of what we have to do on the way back," Landon said. "We can't leave anything that could be traced back to us. They'll search for us on the north side of the road because now they will think we tried to escape in that direction. Hopefully that'll buy us enough time to gather our things and head south."

They ran across the roadway into the woods. Landon touched his right hip to make sure the 44 Magnum was still there and then followed the others back toward the mine site. They were relieved to see that their backpacks and rifle were still where they'd left them. Stone winced as he reached down to grab his pack, and then straightened and reached with his left hand instead.

They ran back down the trail alongside the creek, this time not taking the time to cover tracks or make sure they were being quiet. About a kilometre later they slowed to a fast walk and then slowed to a sustainable pace. They didn't stop until they reached the spot where they'd had lunch earlier.

Kirsten called to Bob who came, tail wagging. She wrapped her arms around his neck.

"You are such a brave boy. My hero."

She grinned at Landon. "He saved my life, you know." Then she giggled. "You should've seen the look on their faces when that truck was headed toward them. How on earth did you know it would start?"

The dog moved over and lay beside Landon, happy to have his owner's hand running down his side.

"I didn't. I had no way of knowing; I jumped into the cab and noticed the keys in the ignition so gave it a try. Thank God it worked. Otherwise I would have had to use my handgun. I do hope they're both going to recover though. I don't want to be responsible for any deaths."

Stone stared at Kirsten. "And you!" he began. "What were you thinking? You could have been killed. You need to talk this stuff over with us. Don't just take off on your own. I was…"

Kirsten raised her hand to silence him. "And if I did talk it over with you, would you have let me go ahead and do it? Don't answer that. You and I both know what the answer is. We were in this together but the two of you started treating me like I wasn't capable of helping. Well, I'm very capable, and now you know it too."

Stone hesitated and then resigned himself to her position.

She smiled and reached over and touched Stone's arm. He pulled his hand away with an involuntary reflex. Landon stepped over and lifted Stone's arm. His right hand was swollen and discoloured.

"Looks like you've done some damage to that hand," he said. He passed a crumpled piece of paper to Stone. "Here, this was in the Hummer."

"Yeah. I think I broke something on that jerk's face. In the movies they don't show you that your hand can get smashed when you hit someone," Stone grimaced. "Damn."

He lifted the scrap of paper that Landon had given him. It was the top left-hand corner of a piece of letterhead with the name *GroundSave Mining Corporation* emblazoned on it.

Kirsten moved over to inspect his damaged hand. "We need to get you to the hospital."

"I'm not sure if that's a good idea," said Stone. "I'd have to have a good cover story to explain it, especially if word gets out about this little fiasco."

Landon inspected his rifle and handgun, then moved beside the other two.

"We'll think of something," he said as he glanced down at Stone's hand. "You will have to see a doctor though, just to be safe."

He slipped the 44 back into its holster and slung the Winchester onto his back. They grabbed their packs and started the trek toward Fish Lake and safety.

Melody Lloyd slammed the receiver of the phone into the cradle. She stood abruptly, pushing her chair to the wall with the backs of her knees. Her lips were pressed tightly together as she breathed heavily through her nose. She walked over to the glass wall in her office that overlooked the Yukon River. Then she whirled around, kicking a trashcan through the air.

"How the hell could something this stupid happen?" She glared at her vice-president. "Were those fucking guards asleep on the job? That was supposed to be a low-profile operation."

As Corporate President for the GroundSave Mining Corporation, it was her job to make sure that shareholders continued to see a profit in the mining and exploration that the company was involved in. Having someone overtake employees and mow down the gatekeepers' building was something she didn't want to have to explain to them.

Tom Alexander sat in the stiff-backed upholstered chair facing her desk and stared straight ahead, his hands fidgeting and wringing. It felt like he was still a child being chastised by his mother.

"I really don't know, Mel. We've done everything we can to keep the operation from becoming any more public than is legally required. We've had absolutely no issues up to this point. Maybe it's only a fluke accident."

"You better get your ass in gear fixing this so-called accident or you can kiss your cushy vice-president in charge of public relations job goodbye. I don't want this becoming a matter of public discussion, and I certainly don't want it hitting the news."

She moved over and rested her derrière on the front of her desk as she leaned forward into Alexander's face. "You got that?"

Alexander's eyes opened wide as he pressed back into the chair.

"There's no reason for it to become public at all. There's nothing going on there to attract people's attention. It had to be someone who's trying to steal from the project." He started wiping his palms on his thighs.

"You never mentioned that anything was stolen. What was stolen?"

"Well, actually, nothing that we know of...but maybe that's because they were caught before they got anything."

"God, you better be right. I'm going to shut down that fucking operation for a while and wait for this to blow over. Now get the hell out there and make sure nothing more happens."

Alexander scurried out of the room, pushing the door closed behind him. A flood of relief washed over him as he heard it click shut. He punched the elevator button several times, then running out of patience, opened the door to the stairwell and ran down the two flights to the bottom.

He stood in the hallway wiping the sweat from his forehead and trying to clear his mind so he could think of what to do next. He crossed his arms across his chest and leaned back against the wall, his eyes closed. *God, she's such a bitch*, he thought as images of his mother and of Melody Lloyd blurred across each other in his mind.

"Something I can help you with?" He opened his eyes to see a middle-aged woman in office attire frowning at him.

"No, nothing!" he barked at her.

He was immediately embarrassed by his outburst and took a deep breath. "I'm sorry I snapped at you," he began in a soft-spoken voice. "I'm looking for the personnel office. It's on this floor, isn't it?"

"Yes, Sir, it is," she said as she pressed herself against the other side of the hall, her eyes darting to the far end of the corridor. "It's at the far end of the building."

Get a hold of yourself, Tom, he thought as he walked through the glass door marked *Human Resources*. A young woman in horn-rimmed glasses and hair done up in a bun raised her eyes from her desk and came to the counter.

"How can I help you, Sir?"

Jesus, he thought, *these people don't even know who I am. Fuck! Nothing has changed since I was a kid. I am the goddamn Corporate Vice President in Charge of Public Relations, you idiot!*

He inhaled deeply before answering. "My name is Tom Alexander. I am the Vice President in Charge of Public Relations. I want to talk to somebody about doing some hiring. Actually, I want to talk to the chief personnel officer. Please tell him I'm here."

She backed away from the counter and turned to open the door to one of the inner offices. After a short discussion with the man inside, she came back to the counter and opened the gate to let Alexander through. She led him to the office and introduced him.

"This is Vice-President Tom Alexander, Sir. He wants to speak with you."

The man rose from behind his desk and extended his right hand in greeting.

"Welcome, Mr. Alexander. It's nice to meet you. I'm the chief personnel officer. My name is Doyle. Paddy Doyle."

Chapter 7

Brad slid his chair back and motioned toward the holograph screen that sat on the table in the garage. "The stats are impressive although rather disconcerting," he said. "Have a look."

Charles and Galen carried their coffees over to the desk where Brad was sitting. He had brought a Virtual Portable Computer from work home to the Fleming residence—after telling his supervisor that there were some problems with it that he wanted to work on. The solid-state memory was loaded with data from The Coalition's information system.

"You'll have to decipher all this for me," said Galen. "It just looks like a jumble of numbers on a map to me." His smile belied the fact that although he was fully capable of understanding the data before him, he was aware that Charles, as a man who had not spent time with electronics, would find the mass of information bewildering. Charles was a man of the earth.

Brad stood and motioned for Galen to sit at the chair. He and Charles leaned over the old man's shoulders.

"The first map shows the number of mines that were operating back before the turn of the Century— between 1975 and 1999," Brad began interpreting the data. "The blue letters indicate the ones that were new during that time. The notes at the bottom indicate that there were less than 190 mines and exploration companies working in Yukon at that time. On the next page it shows an increase to 213 by 2012."

Galen lifted his head to see Brad. "I don't see anything about oil and gas companies."

"There wasn't much going on there until an agreement between Yukon and China took place in 2012. After that, a company from Calgary, 60% foreign owned, began explorations up in Eagle Plains."

Charles leaned forward, focused on the screen. "What took so long for them to get started on the oil and gas? There's sure a hell of a lot of them working up here now."

"Regulations," answered Galen. "The regulations that were put in place between 1998 and 2008 were cost prohibitive and restrictive—plus the First Nations were entitled to royalties and could say no to any wells on their traditional land. Then, changes to the regulations in 2014 removed the First Nations' veto power to oil and gas development and opened southern Yukon up for fracking."

"And don't forget," Brad chimed in, "there was *The Agreement*. Remember, Dad? The federal government signed an agreement in 2012 that gave foreign companies—in that specific instance, China—the right to own and operate mines and resource extraction companies in Canada without the restrictions of having to comply with Canadian regulations, rules and laws…at least that was the end result of allowing them to sue if any government introduced enactments that interfered with their profits so governments left them alone."

Galen raised his head, first turning to Charles and then to Brad. "I can imagine what happened after that," he said.

Brad reached forward and motioned with his finger to scroll to the next page. Galen sat back in the chair, his head cocked to one side; Charles stood erect, his eyes wide as he gazed down at the VPC's hologram screen.

After what appeared to be an eternity of silence, Brad said, "Quite a change, isn't it?"

The new map was covered in red, blue, and green numbers instead of simply naming the companies in each location. According to the legend on the map, the red numbers were mines that had exhausted their resources or were otherwise shut down, the blue were active mines and the green were oil and gas activities. A list of the companies corresponding to the numbers was on the following page.

"This map shows the current status of mining and gas and oil work," said Brad.

"Jesus, there's that many mines and gas companies working up here?" Charles was incredulous.

"Not all of them will be actively mining or drilling," said Galen. "This map also shows the areas where exploration is taking place. It simply indicates spots where work of some kind is going on. History shows that the majority of mines were quite conscientious about protecting the environment and treated their employees well. The stringent regulations became necessary in order to deal with the few who were not. Unfortunately, in the period following *The Agreement*, the few became the many. You see, local corporations could no longer compete with multinationals that could bring in workers from other countries and not have to adhere to any of the environmental standards or, for that matter, labour standards or safety requirements. Most Canadian companies have moved their operations elsewhere."

"I had no idea there was so much work going on that close to Whitehorse," said Charles as he narrowed his gaze. "I'm guessing that most of it was exploration and that there's actually very little mining taking place that close to a populated area."

Galen slowly shook his head. "There's no way of knowing from this map, but if there is mining activity in the vicinity, I expect they'll try to keep it as quiet as possible, especially if they're not being careful with the environment."

Brad pointed at the asterisk beside several of the green numbers. "See that asterisk? That shows the locations where the oil and gas companies used, or are using, fracking as a method to extract the gas." He turned so he could see both the other men. "Remember fracking? Forcing fluids between layers of rock in order to split them apart and allow access to the gas and oil beneath them? Do you notice anything interesting about where they are all located?"

Charles and Galen studied the map, now anxious to see where the asterisks were located. A number were found in the Tintina Trench area, but the majority were in southern Yukon from slightly north of Whitehorse all the way down to Watson Lake. The Whitehorse trough was littered with them.

"Those bastards! Assholes!" said Galen. Both Brad and Charles were taken aback by the sudden, uncharacteristic outburst. "It's no wonder they had to stop everyone from using water other than what they're supplying us. They've polluted the majority of the water table in the entire southern Yukon."

He turned in the chair to face Charles and Brad.

"They were told that's what would happen," he continued. "They were told that fracking would contaminate groundwater and even cause problems with air quality. It allows gases and hydraulic fracturing chemicals to be released into the air. They were told that spills and carelessness would cause contamination of the soil. But they didn't pay any attention. They ignored all of the scientific advice they were given, all in the name of profit. That damned Agreement has them so afraid, they're willing to risk life itself rather than end up in arbitration. We're damn lucky we haven't had any earthquakes."

Charles straightened, turned and walked over to the window facing his yard. He stood, staring out the window, motionless. Brad moved to his father's side. Charles turned to him, his face tight and his eyes flashing with anger through the gathering tears.

"We have to do something. We can't sit by any longer. This has gotten to be a matter of life and death."

Galen took a deep breath to calm himself. "It always was," he said. "But nobody wanted to accept that."

The two younger men felt the warmth in Galen's gentle eyes as he continued. "But, yes, it is definitely time. The question is what to do and how to go about it. We need to gather more like-minded people together. It will be difficult. Remember, it's now a capital offence to be seen as conspirators against The Coalition. That's going to scare a lot of people off."

They were startled by the jangling of the old pushbutton phone sitting on the shelf by the door. Charles strode over and picked up the receiver.

He listened as the familiar voice on the other end said, "Charles, this is Nora. There's been a break-in at a mine near Whitehorse."

"Near Whitehorse?" he asked. Nora confirmed that the action had taken place very near the capital city and that the culprits had not been located as yet. Galen gave a thumbs-up to the other two men.

"We're not alone," he smiled.

The exterior of the Whitehorse General Hospital was horribly stained and in need of paint. Like so many others across the country, it hadn't been properly maintained for the last couple of decades. The automatic doors no longer worked so Kirsten pushed them open to allow Stone through. Landon had taken Bob back to their cabin for some rest and rejuvenation. Stone's hand throbbed inside the ice pack as he made his way past the counter that used to house the receptionists and headed toward Emergency.

"I hope we're doing the right thing," he said to Kirsten. "I still don't know what to give them as a reason for the injury."

"You'll think of something," Kirsten said as they reached the end of the corridor, and found no one at the Emergency desk, only a sign saying to wait. "You have to have that hand looked after or it's going to become completely useless. I'll come in with you. We'll figure something out."

They remained in the waiting area for about half an hour, taking turns pacing back and forth in front of the old television sets that no longer worked.

"I remember when I was a kid," Stone said, "this place was still like new and was filled with people that worked here." He pointed toward the entrance. "There used to be receptionists that took your information and directed where you needed to go. It's gone downhill so quickly."

Kirsten was standing behind him with her hands on his shoulders when the nurse stepped through the Emergency Room door. She appeared to be a very efficient, no-nonsense kind of woman. She was wearing light blue scrubs and comfortable shoes—her tightly-pinned salt-and-pepper hair completed the look. Stone's eyes dropped to the name tag on her left lapel. It read *Nora Walsh, R.N.*

Nora waved at them to come through the door into the Emergency area. She led them into a room immediately on their left and, after noticing that Stone was favouring his right hand, suggested he have a seat.

"Sorry for the wait," she said. "So, what do we have here?"

"I hurt my hand."

"Okay, so...how did it happen?"

"Um, I was working on a car and the wrench slipped... and I hit my hand on the bumper." Stone winced, realizing that he had given a weak explanation of the injury. It was too late to change his story now so he'd have to stick with it.

"A bumper eh? Looks like you hit your *bumper* quite hard. Are you in a lot of pain?" Stone nodded as Nora took his pulse and hooked up the blood pressure monitor. "Are you allergic to anything?"

"No, not that I know of."

Nora carefully unwrapped the ice pack from his right hand. She frowned at the extreme discolouration and swelling. "How long ago did this happen?"

"About eight hours ago."

"Why did you take so long to get here?"

"Um, I decided to wait until Kirsten could drive me here." He locked on to Nora's eyes. "I was afraid I wouldn't be able to drive safely." Her look softened.

"Well, first things first. Come this way." Nora guided him to one of the gurneys behind a well-worn set of drapes hanging above its foot. Kirsten padded silently behind them.

After helping Stone get settled on the bed, Nora turned to leave the examining room. "I'll have a doctor here as quickly as possible," she said as she drew the curtains closed.

Kirsten rolled a stool over and sat near the head of the bed and stroked Stone's forehead. She was careful not to touch his arm or hand.

"That was some pretty fast thinking," she snickered quietly. "Working on the car and slamming your fist into a bumper. Yup, some pretty fast thinking."

Stone grinned sheepishly and started to roll toward her. The move caused him to grimace and quickly lay flat on his back with his elbow on the mattress and his hand elevated. "Mmm, that smarted. I really don't think she bought the story but there's nothing I can do about that now. I hope they're able to fix the hand so I can get out here."

Kirsten stood and leaned over him to kiss his perspiring forehead. "Are you feeling hot? You're sweating a lot."

The screen was abruptly yanked open and a man in green scrubs and a multi-coloured hospital gown stood looking at them.

"So this is the man that punches the bumper of the car," he said with a grin and a French accent. "Dr. Archibeque at your service," he added with a slight nod. "You can call me Matt."

He moved beside the examination bed and carefully lifted Stone's right arm. "That's some nasty bruising. I'll get an x-ray done to see if anything is broken before we decide what to do." He turned his eyes to Kirsten. "I'll be back in a little bit."

The x-ray was completed by an unkempt man who gave the impression that he had better things to do than to be looking after patients. Stone was returned to the curtained off examining room where Kirsten still waited.

"I can't believe how badly this place has deteriorated," Stone muttered, shaking his head. "It's so sad. At least the nurse and the doctor in here seem to care about what they're doing." He sat on the edge of the bed holding his right elbow in his left hand in order to keep the injured hand raised to stop the pounding ache.

"Good news!" said Matt as he yanked the curtain aside, causing both Kirsten and Stone to jump. "Nothing's broken. You have some nasty bruising in that hand, but that's all. I want you to keep icing it for 15 minutes every couple of hours and I'll give you a prescription for an anti-inflammatory. You should be back to normal within a couple weeks."

Matt motioned to the counter where Nora was completing charts. She came to the examining area where Stone and Kirsten waited. She handed the doctor Stone's chart.

"You remember the police telling us about the attempted break-in at the mine," the doctor began. "This injury is probably one that should be reported, don't you think?"

"I, I, I'm not really sure, Sir," she stammered. "We don't have to report every injury that comes in here. I don't think this one is that much different from any other." Her eyes darted among the faces of the three.

Matt turned to observe his patient. His mind wandered back to his childhood and a vague recollection of a woman in Hinkley, California who had taken on an oil company—and beat them—after they had poisoned the water in their community. His recollection of the horror of what had happened to the citizens in that area disturbed him. He repeated what he had told Stone and then handed the clipboard and chart back to her, looking directly into her eyes. "He's very lucky that when the car slipped off the jack and the tire landed on his hand that it didn't crush it entirely."

Nora frowned at him questioningly. "But, that's not what…"

He maintained his gaze. "I said, he's very lucky that when the car slipped off the jack and the tire landed on his hand that it didn't crush it entirely."

Her eyes dropped to the chart. She could see that the one that she had filled out had been replaced by one in the doctor's handwriting. It now read that a slipping jack and a tire landing on Stone's hand was the reason for the injury. She raised her eyes to meet his again.

"If you need me I'll be in the doctor's lounge," he grinned.

Nora breathed a sigh of relief as the doctor walked away. He was mumbling something about how no one would believe that Stone punched a bumper. She turned to Kirsten and Stone while pulling the drape closed behind her.

"It's obvious that the only way that hand could be injured the way it is would be by punching something, or someone. Now, I'm not sure exactly what you're up to, but you're getting the benefit of the doubt and the records here will show something different. You heard what the doctor said to say was the cause. I have my own suspicions. You dropped this in the waiting area," she said as she handed him a wrinkled piece of paper. It was the letterhead remnant from the GroundSave Mining Corporation that Landon had given him.

He was unsure what to expect next. "Thank you. Thank you for everything," he said as he waited to see if she had more to tell him.

Nora turned and handed Kirsten a small bottle with six Naproxen as well as a prescription for several more.

"He's to take one every 12 hours until the prescription is all used up. Use ice on the hand every couple of hours like the doctor said for the next two or three days and be careful in order to allow the hand to heal."

"Thank you. I'll make sure he follows your instructions," Kirsten said as she took the medication from Nora, taking an extra couple of seconds to hold her hands.

Nora turned and grasped the curtain. She stopped and turned on her heel to face them. "I understand there's going to be a town hall meeting soon about the situation with water and the various health implications that have arisen over the past few years. Maybe the two of you would be interested in coming."

She reached into the pocket of her uniform and handed them a card. It read, *Nora Walsh, Humanitarian. 867-555-6672.*

Chapter 8

Melody Lloyd rose from her desk and walked across the office to the washroom. She stood in front of the mirror inspecting her makeup and coiffure, making sure that nothing about her appearance was amiss. Her light gray pantsuit gave her the appearance of being both well-dressed and businesslike. The only thing that seemed out of place was the garish, bright red lipstick that she was never seen without.

She returned to her glass-topped desk to fetch the folder that was sitting by the phone. *I guess they've stewed long enough*, she thought as she strode across the floor and opened the door to the conference room. Lloyd always made a point of having others wait for her.

"I'm glad to see you could all make it," she said, sweeping her eyes across the room at the four men. "We have some things to discuss."

Wolfgang Grimm and Tom Alexander stood as she walked through the door. Across the expanse of the table, Sam Chong remained seated with his hands clasped in front of him, his thumbs rolling over each other. Josef Poste, who was sitting beside him, ran to the head of the large conference table and rolled the chair away from the wooden top so Lloyd could sit.

Lloyd ignored the seat being held by Poste and went directly to the chair he had vacated beside Chong.

"I expect you've all heard about the incident at our Whitehorse location? I've asked you to come here so we can make sure that something like this never happens again."

Chong turned his chair toward her and then back to the other two across the broad tabletop. He then turned his attention back to Lloyd. "I only have a small amount of information about this. My understanding is that nothing was taken and no damage done. Is that correct?"

She squirmed in her chair as if trying to find a comfortable position then opened the folder that was on her lap and shuffled the papers. She had always felt uncomfortable around Sam Chong.

"Yes, that is correct," she said. "Nothing taken, no damage. It makes me wonder why they bothered to break-in in the first place though. I'm also concerned about what appears to be a lack of security at the site."

"The entire area is surrounded by fencing and razor wire," said Alexander, glancing over at Poste. "There were two guards on duty that night and no apparent reason to explain how they got in."

"Has the fence been inspected for damage?" Lloyd directed her question at the small, bald man who was sitting at the front edge of his chair, his arms on the table with his elbows held out in an attempt to appear larger than he was.

Poste sank back in the chair that appeared over-sized with him in it. "I don't think there's been time yet," he choked in a barely audible voice.

Chong's upper lip curled. "Well, make time, you little ferret. Have it done by the end of today." He turned back to Lloyd. "Were the security guards employees of the company or contracted out?"

Both Lloyd and Grimm slowly turned their eyes to Poste as he attempted to disappear even further into the back of the chair.

"They were employees of my security company," Poste said. "Top-notch, dependable men. I'd stake my reputation on them."

"You already have, and they let you down," said Chong. "We need to make sure that everyone knows that they cannot interfere with the workings of mines and other businesses. After all, they should know that it is those corporations that employ them and keep the economy strong."

He stood and walked to the head of the table, leaned forward on his hands and scrutinized each person in the room. "So, what suggestions do you have?"

Lloyd raised her eyes to him, her hands still toying with the folder in front of her. "We could make an example of the people who did this…as soon as we find out who they are."

"Don't be stupid," growled Chong. "There's no time to try and figure out who the hell it was that broke into your fucking mine. We need to make them understand now."

Grimm continued staring straight across the table, his brow furrowed and his eyes unfocused. "I don't see how we can do that without finding out who broke in. We can't charge somebody without some kind of proof. And we certainly can't punish somebody without knowing they did it, can we?"

"Stop telling me what we can't do!" Chong slammed his open hands on the table. "Think of some goddamn solutions."

"There's always the new punishment section in the Criminal Code," Lloyd said. "I never thought there would be a reason to use it but I'm starting to see now why The Coalition wanted it included."

The statement got Grimm's attention. "What new section is that? I don't remember any changes to the Criminal Code being talked about in Parliament."

Lloyd grinned knowingly. "Most people missed it because there was no discussion. It was buried in the last 500 or so page Omnibus Bill. It brings back public Corporal Punishment for some offences. Things like providing water from an unapproved source are included as offences where this punishment can be invoked. Conspiring against The Coalition is now considered treason as well."

Grimm sat back in his seat, wide-eyed. "You're not serious. Are you talking about something like a public flogging? You can't be serious. They couldn't have passed that."

"Oh, but they did," she continued. "And if we find the bastards that did this I think it would be a great sentence. It would certainly dissuade others from trying the same thing."

Lloyd focused on the back of her hands, inspecting her manicure. She stood and walked to the file cabinet in the corner of the room, her heels sinking into the thick carpet making the movement appear clumsy. She returned with a set of three-ring binders, four in all.

"This is the Bill I was talking about. It has been passed in its entirety with no amendments." She opened the second volume, turning to page 327. "There it is; section 932, complete with a list of offences that are punishable by public Corporal Punishment."

Poste jumped out of his chair and moved around to her side. He read the section she was referring to, running his finger under each word as he went along. "Well, I'll be damned. Now we can teach those worthless bastards something. We can show them who's in charge."

Chong reached back and pulled the high-backed leather chair up to the table. "That still involves finding someone and convicting them," he said as he settled at the head of the table. "We need something more immediate than that. Poste, what do you have to say?"

"I don't know," Poste stammered. "I don't know what we can do. Unless we catch somebody breaking the law or convict them after a trial, there's not much we can do. Is there?"

"That still leaves us with the problem of finding out who they were," said Grimm.

"Not really," snapped Chong. "If people know what to expect they won't cross the line anymore. This little man was right," he said indicating Poste. "They need to know who is in control."

Poste rushed past Lloyd toward Chong. "What do you think we should do? What's your idea?" He was so intent on pleasing Chong, he was panting like a little puppy.

When Poste was within reach, Chong backhanded him across the side of the face, dropping him to the floor.

Lloyd sat emotionless as Grimm leaped to his feet. "What the hell was that about? You can't come here and treat people like that!"

Chong remained motionless, staring down at the crumpled Poste. "You understand, don't you?" he said scornfully. "You appreciate what I'm getting across to you, right?" Chong was a strong believer that fear was an effective method of control.

Poste drew his legs close to his body, turned his face to the floor, and nodded. He knew what to do; he knew how to keep people under control. *That son of a bitch,*

83

nobody treats me like that and gets away with it, he thought. Meanwhile, he remained curled up on the floor.

Chong sneered down at him, and then turned to Lloyd. "You might want to consider getting some real security for your mine sites."

Nora stopped halfway across the Robert Campbell Bridge over the Yukon River toward downtown Whitehorse to lean over the rail and watch, unseeing, as the water flowed by. She often made this walk from her home in Riverdale; a walk that would take her to the old Rotary Park then around the old Millennium Trail in a complete circle. Her mind was filled with questions. She wondered how far things would go before people would finally revolt and demand change from The Coalition. How much damage would take place in her beloved Yukon before it would come to an end? But most of all, on this day, her biggest question was how the little girl Keira had gotten enough poison in her system to kill her. The last ten days had not provided any answers.

She collected herself and continued to walk to the end of the bridge where, turning right, she took the path back under the bridge to start heading south on the well-worn, paved trail. She set her gaze at the crumbling hulk of what used to be a national treasure, the S.S. Klondike sternwheeler. It hadn't been maintained since the federal government cutbacks of 2012 and because it was incapable of generating large amounts of income, The Coalition would not operate it as a museum the way it had been prior to that.

Such a shame, she thought, *history lost*. She remembered being taken through the boat on a tour when she arrived in Whitehorse in 2010. The paddle wheel that drove the vessel upstream and was such a bright orange, reflecting sunlight or dripping with dew, was now lying partially sunk in the sand as one side had fallen. The period furniture and artifacts that had once graced the upper and lower decks had long been ransacked and everything pilfered, leaving the wooden planks barren and open to weathering and decay.

The sun was warm on her face as she followed the trail to where it turned into the woodland that led to a footbridge taking her back to the other side of the river. Once across, she decided to continue her walk and turned north on that part of the trail that would take her back to the Robert Campbell Bridge.

She smiled as a family with three young children walked toward her, the kids laughing and running back and forth. On her left, about 50 metres away, a man sat on one of the memorial benches facing the river with a dog at his feet. She felt her emotions rise within her as she observed a scene that used to be commonplace.

As she rounded the next corner of the path she realized that she recognized the man on the bench. She left the pavement and walked toward the river and back on a dirt path that would lead her in front of the bench where the man sat.

"Good morning," she sang out as she approached them. "It's a beautiful day, isn't it?" She knelt down and placed her hand in front of the husky/shepherd cross who had now risen to a sitting position. She started to stroke the top of his head. "Lovely dog."

Landon glanced at her with little interest and then returned his gaze over the flowing water. "He's a good dog."

Nora stood up and moved over to the bench and sat down. "My name is Nora Walsh," she said as she reached her right hand out to shake his.

Landon frowned, and then returned the gesture, clasping her hand in his. "Landon. This here's Bob." He released his grip and returned his gaze to the water.

"I've seen you before." Nora leaned forward and turned to him, trying to catch his eye.

His eyes flicked toward her but his body and head remained motionless. "Is that so?"

"Yes. At the hospital. I am a nurse in Emergency and I was on duty when you brought that little girl in a while back. I am so very sorry," she said quietly as she turned straight on the bench.

He sat still for a moment then turned toward her. "Is there something I can do for you?" he asked impatiently.

"No. I just thought I would say hello and introduce myself." She leaned back on the bench as they both sat watching the water flow by. Several moments of quiet elapsed.

Nora broke the silence. "I remember when this trail used to have lots of people using it, and the river would be flooded with kayakers and canoeists. Things have changed so much in such a short time, don't you think?"

"Lady, I appreciate you stopping to chat but I'm not a real sociable fellow."

"It's Nora," she said. "And you and I have a lot more to talk about than you think."

Landon's attention was piqued as he turned toward her. "Such as?"

"Oh, the environment, water, the way we are all being treated by government and The Coalition," she smiled.

"Lady, that kind of talk gets people in a lot of trouble these days, especially when you are talking about The Coalition."

"Yes, I know. Don't you find it irritating that we're not allowed to have an opinion on how things are run any longer?"

"Look, Lady—"

"Nora."

"Nora…I don't want to get involved in anything, period. I've had enough shit with the authorities and don't want any more. I really don't want to get tangled up in anything."

"And yet you drop everything to bring a sick little girl to the hospital," Nora observed gently.

"She died." Landon's eyes began to fill.

"Yes. But not through any fault of yours. You did everything that could possibly be done. Did you know that some of us suspect the water in the creek she drank from is tainted?"

"Of course it is. That damn mine—" Landon stopped and turned away from her.

"Ah, so you know about the mine. We recently had a young man come in for treatment of his hand and I figured out that he was involved in the incident at the mine. We decided not to report his injury and to give him a cover story."

Landon turned back to her, his body tense. "Why would you do that?"

"Not everyone is willing sheep. There is a movement afoot—"

His muscles relaxed as he let out a long-held breath. "I was with them," he let slip. Nora was surprised that he offered the information.

Bob stood up, went to Nora and placed his head in her lap. She used both hands to scratch behind his ears. His eyes closed and his tail wagged contentedly.

Landon watched, thinking that she must be OK for Bob to take to her the way he did.

"You say we have a lot to talk about? I take it that means you are going to talk and you expect me to listen? You should know up front that I don't get talked into things. I think you'd be wasting your time."

Nora smiled and reached over to pat his hand, then allowed hers to rest easily on his. "Nothing of the kind. I kind of thought we'd share some insights and thoughts on things."

He gently withdrew his hand and rubbed the back of his neck.

OK, he doesn't want to be touched, Nora thought as she turned to face the river again. *Remember that.* "I gather you've lived here a long time?" she asked.

"Since '92. Used to work in mining exploration."

"I came in 2010. Are you retired?"

"Naw, I decided to stop doing it. The rules changed and the foreign companies came in. There was no respect being given to the land and I didn't want to be part of that so I quit."

"So, you are an environmentalist then?"

Landon leaned toward her. "If you mean one of those idiots that babble on about how everything needs to come to a halt in the name of the 'environment,' then no, I'm not. Those hypocrites get in their cars or planes and travel around the world burning up the fossil fuels, all the while proclaiming they are protecting the environment. No, I'm not one of them."

She was taken aback by the emotion he expressed.

He sat back and continued. "But if you are asking if I am someone who wants to see the extraction of resources done in a respectful manner that mitigates damage as much as possible, then I would probably fall into that category. Which one do you fall under?"

Nora laughed. "You don't leave any confusion as to what your opinion is, do you? I would have to say that my views correspond with yours. But, in the meantime, The Coalition and their corporate partners are wreaking havoc over our entire country. Some of us believe they must be stopped."

"Like I said, Nora, I really don't want to get involved. The way I see it, humans are the only creatures that ever existed that are willing to kill themselves and others over something completely imaginary, like money and power. Believe me; I don't want to get involved."

"Too many people don't want to get involved," Nora bristled. She closed her eyes and breathed deeply. "We really need to have level-headed, reasonable folks coming forward," she said, trying to persuade him.

"Well, I'm not your guy."

Nora stood and trained her eyes down at him. "I'm sorry to hear you say that," she said and then turned and sped toward the asphalt trail.

As Landon turned to watch her leave, a glint of sunlight reflected from the bench, catching his eye. He read the memorial plaque. *Wenda McGuire. She loved this land and its people.*

He recalled walking along this same trail with his wife as she marvelled at the forest, river and sky. He remembered listening to her as she talked about the hope and wishes she had for her fellow Yukoners and Canadians. He could feel her presence.

Landon squinted through the trees at the receding image of the woman he had sent away only a moment before.

"Nora!" he shouted. "Nora!"

She stopped and turned back to look at him.

"Wait up!" he yelled as he waved at her. He patted the plaque and grinned ironically as he struck out toward Nora.

A slap on his thigh brought his dog to his side. "Come on, Bob. We have things to do."

Chapter 9

Danielle turned back down the trail to watch as her wife stopped hiking to lean on her walking poles and catch her breath. Danielle was impressed with Sherry's willingness to accompany her on hikes, even one this long. The Tors was an arduous climb, but still relatively close to Whitehorse. For experienced climbers, it was an eight-hour round trip. But for the two of them it would be closer to twelve.

"Come on, Honey, you're almost here."

Sherry gawked at the distance up the hill, and then back down at her feet. She straightened and enjoyed the rock formations and the view of the Kluane Mountains to the west. She reached out with her right pole and began her final ascent with her left foot. A few minutes later she reached Danielle and the two of them hugged, kissed and then stood side by side admiring the vista.

Sherry was fascinated by the panorama before them. The mountains and valleys formed by the Aishihik and Dezadeash rivers and the forests between them stretched out to infinity.

"Oh my God," she said. "I am so glad you brought me here. I didn't think anything this beautiful was possible."

Danielle put her arm around Sherry's waist and drew her close. "We need to see as much of this kind of thing while we still can. I think more people should get out of town and see what is out here."

"Look," Sherry whispered, as she crouched slightly and pointed to a space between two of the rock formations. "Sheep!"

Danielle's gaze followed Sherry's finger and they watched as a large ram stepped up beside the ewe they had first spotted. The sheep stopped and observed the two women and then quietly turned and melted from view.

"Wow!" said Sherry as she stood watching in wonderment across the small plateau to where the animals had stood; their dematerialization seemingly mystical.

Danielle smiled as she broke the silence. "Should we have a look around before we have something to eat or would you like to eat first?" she asked.

"I think I'd like to just sit for a while."

Danielle was the first to notice the gray toque as it bobbed along the edge of the hillside moving east. She nudged Sherry and nodded her head in the direction of the movement. A moment later, the toque rose further to unveil a man's head, shoulders, legs and eventually his entire body as he moved up the trail toward them. His movements were unhurried and he appeared to be very stable and sure of himself as he hiked up the narrow trail. He wore a backpack with a tripod hanging from it and placed his walking poles solidly into the turf. When he was about 10 metres away he stopped and gave a small wave.

"Hi, how is your hike been going? It's a beautiful day for it."

Danielle was pleased to hear his French accent. For some reason it made her feel a little safer, as if they had something in common. Even so, she took a step forward and moved a little bit in front of Sherry.

"It's a long way up here, but definitely worth the effort once you're here," she responded.

The man leaned on his poles and took in the view from right to left, then turned back to Danielle and Sherry. "It sure is. I haven't been this way for a long time but I'm glad I came today, it is beautiful. The light later on will be stunning."

Sherry peered around from behind Danielle and spied the tripod on the man's backpack. "Are you a photographer? I see a tripod."

"I always carry a camera with me. I love to capture the wonder of the Yukon wilderness anytime I can," the man said.

There was a moment of awkward silence before he continued, "I guess I'll keep going. I like to see what's over the next mountain. Have yourselves a good day." He stepped off the worn path to walk around them and continue on to the next hillside.

Sherry couldn't contain herself any longer. "I'm Sherry...and this is Danielle," she said as she stepped forward.

Danielle frowned at her but Sherry continued, "We're about to have lunch, would you like to join us?"

He stopped and turned back to them. "That would be nice. But I do not want to impose—or make either of you feel uncomfortable."

"You're more than welcome. Come, sit," Sherry bubbled.

"And you are okay with this too?" He caught Danielle's eye.

"It's part of why I love her so much," Danielle smiled. "She's a gregarious little one. I'd probably not meet anybody if wasn't for her."

"Well, thank you. I could use a break and little company would be nice." He reached out to shake their hands. "I am Gérard Ponthieux. It is very nice to meet you."

Sherry's eyes widened as she recognized who he was. Ponthieux was a world-renowned photographer known for his images from the Peel Watershed and Ogilvie Mountains. She had two of his prints hanging in their home.

"You too," she said as she stared at him, awestruck. She gathered her wits about her again. "Don't you usually hang out in the mountains in northern Yukon?"

"When I have the time I like to travel into the Ogilvie Mountains. For me, they are the heart of the Yukon. Even physically. They are located where the heart would be," he smiled. "But these days I do not have time and besides, there is far too much mining activity and oil and gas exploration going on up there now. It is very disturbing."

Danielle watched him as she poured coffee from a thermos. "They're mining and exploring everywhere now. There doesn't seem to be any rules and regulations anymore."

Gérard pulled out a homemade granola bar that he had packed for his hike. "Not since the local government sold out to foreign interests and the federal government signed *The Agreement*. The environment has been taking a beating ever since then. That is why I keep trying to get out as much as I can—before there is nothing left to go to."

Sherry took a drink from a bottle of water. "I read your book. The one you wrote twenty or so years ago. You made some interesting political statements along with your comments on environmental issues back then. Have you changed your mind on any of that at all?"

"Not really," he said as he sat on a rock beside the path. "If anything, what has taken place since then only substantiated my manifesto."

"Do you still think the government then was fascist and not democratic?"

"Democracy is an illusion. If you think back, the government that was ruling Canada between 2011 and 2015 had the power of a majority government with only about 24% of the population supporting them. While they were in power, most of their decisions were made strictly for the benefit of the government rather than for the people, because they had the belief that as long as the government was looked after, the people would be fine. That's a very simple way to describe fascism."

Sherry moved from beside Danielle and sat beside Gérard. "Do you still think it's a fascist government that's running Canada? How do you change things when they make all the rules?"

"No, we do not have a fascist government anymore," he said returning her eye contact. "We are now governed by corporatists. It is Big Business, mostly foreign Big Business that has control of Canada these days." His voice had gotten a little louder and his speech faster. His energy level was elevated.

"Nothing has changed since I wrote that book," he went on. "There is still only one way to bring about change and bring the power to the people—Revolution! Blood must be spilt."

"Jesus, I hope you're wrong," said Danielle. "Hopefully nobody will have to die."

Gérard's eyes burned fiercely as he contemplated the landscape around them that he loved. "People are dying already," he said as he turned back to them. "The way the mines in the oil and gas companies are operating right now is destroying our environment and people are dying from the toxicity. It is already too late to hope nobody will have to die."

Sherry felt sorry that she had brought up the topic of his book, but at the same time felt herself drawn to his ideology. The group who were working toward change could certainly use all the help they could get, but was he too radical to invite?

"Have you ever thought of getting together with other people and working toward change? You know, lobbying, having meetings and getting together in order to request change from government or from The Coalition?" she asked.

Danielle scowled at her.

Gérard shook his head slowly. "No. I don't see how change can take place without eventually leading to violence. As the old saying goes, maybe this is only the beginning of the end."

"I could never think that way," Sherry said softly. "There always has to be hope. As long as we're alive there has to be hope."

"Maybe you are right," he acquiesced. "This is a beautiful day and we're in a wondrous location so let's not worry about the affairs of the world right now. We should enjoy this moment and let the rest look after itself."

Sherry's face lit up and she grinned. "I think you're right."

They finished their meals and the two women packed their gear to start the trek back down the mountains to their car. Gérard hoisted his pack onto his back and, grabbing his walking poles, started heading further into the wilderness. After a few metres he stopped and returned to where Sherry and Danielle waited and watched.

"Thank you for spending some time with an old photographer," he said. "Walk carefully on the way down. I wish you all the best in your journey." He spun around and struck off up the trail.

Sherry raised her hand over her head and waved at him while Danielle watched him retreat until he was out of sight. A tiny flash of colour near the path where they had stopped caught Sherry's attention. She went back, not wanting to leave anything behind in the wilderness. It was a small plastic container holding a digital memory card that had fallen from Gérard's backpack when he pulled out his lunch.

Her eyes went up the trail to where he had disappeared from view. She was about to tell Danielle that they should go after him to give it back, and then she decided it would be a good excuse to get to talk to him again. She slipped it into her pocket and made a mental note to go to his website when she got home.

Stone hit the brakes, causing his little hybrid car to skid to a halt at the edge of the water. He shifted into reverse and backed up about 5 metres. This was the third washout they had come across on the way up to Haeckel Hill, just outside Whitehorse. The road had not been maintained since 2019. He left the Prius and walked over to inspect this latest roadblock.

"It's getting kind of scary trying to get up here," Kirsten said as she opened the passenger door. "I don't think this little car was really intended for this kind of trail."

Stone laughed. "That's for sure. The engineers designing this little baby never thought it would be covering this kind of terrain. I'm glad I saw that big boulder before we drove into it. It was pretty well hidden by the water."

Kirsten walked around the car to see if there was any damage from the last two crossings where creeks had cut their way across the old gravel access road. Seeing none, she walked up to where Stone stood searching for a way through the debased trail.

As she approached he turned and held out his hand. She accepted it then reached for his other hand. They locked eyes as they stood facing each other.

"It's kind of nice to be out here with you, away from everything else," she said. Her eyes glanced back at the flowing water as her lips pursed. "I'm kind of wondering if we're going to be able to make it back."

Stone grinned back at her. "No problem. We'll make it back okay; that is assuming we get there in the first place."

He noticed that Kirsten was more concerned than amused so he pulled her up close and turned toward the washout and pointed into the water.

"I'm only joking, love. See, on this side," he said, pointing toward the right side of the roadway, "the creek bed is stable and shallow enough to drive through."

Kirsten didn't hear anything after the word *love*. Was it a common phrase he used or was he beginning to feel something for her? She enjoyed the warmth of being near him as she felt his strong arm surrounding her shoulders. It was, indeed, quite wonderful to be alone with him, away from all the strife of the city.

"Besides, we only have a couple of kilometres to go before we get to the top," Stone's voice broke into her mesmerizing daydream. "We'll be there in no time."

They returned to the car and climbed inside, buckling up their seatbelts. Stone moved the car slowly forward, inching his way across the water-slicked pebbles until the tires on the front wheel drive grasped dry ground on the other side.

After navigating around several spots where deep ruts would have trapped the small wheels of his little Toyota, they breached the top of the road and parked in the grass and fireweed-overgrown former parking lot. They continued to sit in the car admiring the expanse of the valley with the city of Whitehorse below them and Grey Mountain directly across.

Stone took Kirsten's hand. "It's such a beautiful view from up here. Don't you think?"

"Lovely." Kirsten liked sitting and holding hands with him. During their adventures together she had become quite attached to him.

After spending a few more minutes being quiet together, Stone laid his hand on the door handle. "Okay, let's go do some exploring," he said as he raised the door handle and effortlessly slipped out the open door. Kirsten watched his exit and was impressed with the ease in which he moved. Then she stepped out of the car.

"There's not much left up here that's being cared for," said Stone as his eyes swept across the top of the rise. There were two dilapidated old wind towers, their sides stained with rust and their unmoving propellers showing the beginning of moss growth. The smaller of the two turbines had been installed in 1993 and the larger in 2000 as an experiment in wind-generated power. By 2015, the experiment had been dropped with none of the resulting data being made public.

To the right of the huge windmills was a fenced off area with a couple of small buildings and a 20-metre tall metal tower with an observation deck at its apex. The buildings had once contained communication equipment and other early warning devices but had long ago been broken into, vandalized and subsequently forgotten by the Government, RCMP and The Coalition who were using them.

The rusted tower had been built with much government fanfare in 2014 and was formerly manned by the Wildland Fire Management branch of the Yukon government from May through August each year for forest fire watch. It was abandoned five years later and over a decade and a half had passed since any maintenance had been done on this location. The resulting disintegration of the structures was evident.

Kirsten and Stone eyeballed the more than 100 ladder rungs they would have to climb to get to the top. Stone smiled at Kirsten then looked back up the tower. "It looks like we're going to get a bit of exercise. It's a long way up."

She answered by placing one hiking boot on the first step, grabbing a rung in her hand and beginning to move upward. On the fifth step she heard a creak and a snap. She froze in place, and after a few seconds, continued on her way toward the top.

Several minutes later, she arrived at the landing halfway up the tower with Stone a bit behind her. She slowly pulled herself onto the platform. She glanced down at Stone a couple of metres below.

"Hurry up, we don't have all day," she laughed as he joined her.

"You might want to slow down," he said. "We still have quite a way to go and there's no real rush." He went over to the railing and gazed down. Although they were still only about 10 metres above ground it appeared to be much further. As he leaned out, the railing groaned and began to shift. He jumped back onto the stable platform. "Better stay away from the edge," he said, "this place isn't safe anymore."

They took a few minutes' break before they continued to the banister-encircled platform at the top. The floor had indications of water damage but still seemed to be solid enough to hold them.

Stone moved over to the north side of the platform near Kirsten. She moved in close to him and slid her arm around his waist. Her eyes turned up to him and he leaned forward and, wrapping his arms around her, gave in to the impulse to have his lips find hers. She responded with ardour, opening her mouth slightly to receive his advances. A moment later they parted.

"I wasn't expecting that," Kirsten blushed.

"Neither was I, but you are so beautiful."

The flush on her face became more pronounced as she smiled back at him. "Thank you. You're not so bad yourself," she bubbled. Then she examined the disarray on the floor and turned back to Stone, her face questioning.

"Let's have a look and see if we can find anything unusual before we leave," Stone said. "This place is a mess and I'd like to get you back to town before dark."

She grinned and nodded, then turned back to search over the vast tracts of land they could see from their vantage point.

"Is there anything in particular we are expecting to see?" she asked.

"I don't really know. The mine site will be to the southwest," Stone indicated the direction with his hand. "It must be on the other side of one of those mountains or we would probably be able to see it from here."

Kirsten stared at the wilderness spread before them, searching for anything that might tell her where the mine was. Stone recalled thinking that the road may have started somewhere off the Alaska Highway west of Whitehorse. He suggested that they might be able to find something leading toward the direction of the mine. She narrowed her focus to find anything that might look like a path or roadway through the forest.

She vaguely remembered something about private property so began her examination right at the Alaska Highway. A loop of gravel road off the Alaska Highway had several properties attached to it. "You know what that road is?" she asked, pointing almost directly north from where they were.

"It looks like a section of the old Alaska Highway."

"Are there people living there?"

"Sure. There's a number of properties and acreages along that stretch. There's a road that leads south-west from the north end of that loop that goes up about half a kilometre then forks off to Scout Lake on the left or on to some other properties a few kilometres further in if you go to the right. It goes on for quite a long—"

He stopped talking as if becoming aware of something. They turned toward each other, and then started to laugh.

"That must be it," Kirsten said as she turned to give him a hug. "That must be the road they're using."

102

"It has to be. Of course it does. It has to be," Stone replied excitedly. "Let's get down from here. This place is a mess."

About 30 minutes later, they were seated in the Prius and heading toward town.

"We should get hold of Landon and tell him what we found," Kirsten said. "We're going to need some help in figuring out what to do."

"Yes, I agree, but it's getting kind of late today."

"We'll wait until tomorrow and then call him. In the meantime we should go somewhere and get something to eat," she suggested.

Stone's eyes flickered at her as he drove the little car out of the last of the washouts. "That's a great idea. Where would you like to go?" he smiled.

Kirsten reddened, squeezed his hand, and shyly turned to the side window.

"My place would be fine," she said.

Chapter 10

Town Hall Meeting
Do You Know Your Rights?
Come And Be Part Of The Discussion
We Want To Hear From You
Water – Why Buy From Approved Sources?
Growing Your Own Food – Unsafe?
Mining Regulations
Oil and Gas Regulations
The Coalition – Benefiting You?

7:00 p.m. Saturday, August 23
High Country Inn Meeting Room

Brad Fleming and his friends blanketed downtown Whitehorse with the flyers inviting people to the Town Hall Meeting. They travelled to the suburbs and outlying subdivisions, dropping them into individual mailboxes and leaving them on doorsteps. Charles attempted to do a mail out through Canada Post but they refused to accept the material, saying they were concerned it would be seen as being seditious. The one newspaper that remained in Yukon, *The Coalition Press*, rejected a request to run ads.

Charles and Galen managed to secure a room in the High Country Inn to hold the meeting. The hotel manager was reticent until he checked with President Grimm to see if the hotel would be held liable should the meeting be declared an unlawful assembly. He was advised that both he and his hotel were safe and that he should encourage the organizers of the meeting to proceed. Grimm had preferred that to having the meeting be held in a clandestine manner. At least he would be aware of what was going on.

Mahalia swung the door open and stepped inside Grimm's office. He and Sam Chong were leaning with their elbows on the bar in quiet conversation.

"Ms. Lloyd, Mr. Alexander and Mr. Poste have arrived, Sir," she said to Grimm. Shall I show them in?"

"By all means, Mahalia...and lock the outside door, then come and join us."

Mahalia was incredulous. It was seldom she was privy to any of the information that came out of the meetings with these participants. She was curious why she was being invited this time. She gave him a crooked smile then turned to lock the door.

Once again Grimm was distracted as her fluid movements and form-fitted business suit sashayed out of the room.

Chong gave him a light tap on the shoulder. "Did you hear what I asked you?" Chong's eyes turned toward Mahalia. "Do you always get sidetracked by such simple things? We need you to stay focused."

Grimm flushed slightly. "I was actually thinking about what we were going to talk about today and wasn't listening. I apologize."

Chong stared into his eyes for a moment. "Sure. You are thinking about this meeting. Let's stay with that and get on with it." They moved into the conference room.

Mahalia chaperoned the other three in and invited them to take seats. A pitcher of ice water, surrounded by crystal glasses, was placed at the centre between them.

Chong stood at the head of the table—again. Grimm scowled, finding Chong's arrogance increasingly annoying.

Mahalia sat on one side so Grimm sat beside her. Melody Lloyd and Tom Alexander were across from them. Josef Poste hesitated at the doorway, unsure where to locate himself.

Chong motioned to a chair beside Alexander. "Sit there, Poste. I want you to hear what's going on." Poste lowered his head and moved quietly to where he was told to go.

Chong eyed him for a few seconds then, with a slight shake of his head, sat down. "Mr. Grimm will fill you in. Then we need to decide what to do about it."

Mahalia slid a set of notes in front of Grimm. A quick glance from him betrayed his anxiety. He had talked to her previously about his concerns that The Coalition would someday push people too far and they would fight back. His superiors had scoffed at the idea saying that people would continue to do exactly as they were told, as long as there were laws in place to enforce it. People believed that it was necessary for government and business to be in control, they'd said.

"We received a call from the hotel manager at the High Country Inn," Grimm began. "A group of citizens are renting their large meeting room in order to have a Town Hall Meeting regarding the situation with water, food, mining regulations, oil and gas regulations. But even more intriguing is that they have an item on their agenda about The Coalition, apparently questioning whether it's a good thing for the people."

He removed several copies of the flyer announcing the Town Hall Meeting and distributed them around the table.

Poste leaned his small frame forward and addressed Chong. "I'll take some of my militia and arrest those traitors. We'll show those bastards."

Grimm raised his eyes from the paper in front of him. He didn't like Poste or the way he conducted himself. His preference was to not have Poste included at all.

"Sit down, Mr. Poste. We'll tell you what to do, not the other way around." He made eye contact with each of his guests. "The first question is do we allow this meeting to take place? The second question is how can we turn this to our benefit?"

"I'm not sure why we've been invited to this meeting," said Lloyd. "I really don't see what any of this has to do with my company."

Chong turned his gaze toward her and glared into her eyes. "It was the shit coming from your fucking mine that started all this crap in the first place. Do you think it's a coincidence that this gathering is being organized so soon after your mine site was compromised? Do not question what we do, lady, it will not serve you well. The only reason you are here is so we can tell you what is expected of you."

Lloyd frowned and glared back at him, unused to being spoken to in that manner. She expected some support from Alexander but he averted his eyes. She turned back to Chong.

"Surely, you don't think you can pin the entire country's unrest on one little mining company? I don't know who you think you are but you've been pushing a lot of people around since you got here and I think—"

"Don't think!" Chong interrupted. "I represent The Coalition here. I was sent by The Capitol to clean up some bullshit that has been coming from this area. Bullshit such as mines that don't even bother trying to not poison everything around them. Does that sound familiar?"

"We are owned by a foreign corporation so the regulations don't apply to us! Don't you dare tell me that we're doing something wrong," she retorted.

Chong sat back in his chair with a wry grin. "*The Agreement* does not include allowing the premeditated poisoning of people. The intent was not to allow mines and their owners to commit murder. You allowed concentrated poisons to flow into a stream within 20 kilometres of a populated area. At the very least your company could be found guilty of negligence causing death."

Chong's tone mellowed as he leaned forward on the table. "The reason you are here, Ms. Lloyd, is so we can make sure that none of that happens. And for that, we expect your cooperation—and your respect."

Lloyd retreated back into her chair, chastised. "Why don't we put a stop to the meeting those people are trying to organize?"

Grimm sighed heavily. "If we do that it will only encourage them to go underground and try harder. Furthermore, by letting the Town Hall Meeting take place we will get to know more about who the organizers are and who is supporting them. Of course, if they take it too far it could be seen as a conspiracy against The Coalition."

Poste attempted to speak but was quieted by Grimm's raised hand.

"We will even attend the meeting. All of us," Grimm continued quietly as he exchanged glances with each of them individually. "We will be there in order to assure the public that all is well with the world and that they have nothing to be concerned about."

Chong's gaze moved up the table. "Poste!"

Poste jumped in fright, almost falling off his chair. He gathered himself and directed his full attention toward the head of the table.

Chong lowered his chin slightly and glowered at him. "You are going to bring some of the militia to that meeting to make sure nothing gets out of hand. You will stand at the back of the room and do nothing unless I instruct differently. You will act exactly as I tell you. Do you understand?"

Poste dragged his chair back and stood by the table in an attempt to look and feel larger. "We will make sure everything is safe for you. The militia is at your service, Sir."

Grimm continued handling the documents in front of him but turned his eyes toward Poste. *That little weasel is going to be a problem* he thought. *I hope Chong can control him.*

"So it's agreed then," Grimm said, "we tell the hotel manager to go ahead and book the meeting room and we will all be there."

Melody Lloyd slowly passed her gaze between Grimm and Chong. *I don't think it's really an agreement*, she thought, *it's more like an order I can't get out of.*

"We'll be there," she said, glancing over at Tom Alexander. "We will both be there." Alexander squirmed in his chair as he felt the anxiety of facing the meeting mixed with his fear of Lloyd.

When they were done, Mahalia escorted the visitors out of Grimm's office. She returned to the conference room to find him sitting with his elbows on the table and his head in his hands.

"What is it, Wolfgang?" she asked.

He slowly raised his head from his hands and sat back in his chair. He sought her warm, brown, inviting eyes.

"I'm afraid it's all starting to unravel, Mahalia. I'm very concerned about the way things are going."

She moved over behind his chair and began massaging his shoulders. She swivelled the chair until he was facing her, and then leaned forward and kissed his cheek.

"Everything will be as it's intended to be," she whispered to him. "Everything will be as it's intended to be."

Galen studied the people assembled around him and smiled. They were small in numbers but big in commitment and heart. He was pleased to be a part of their group. The five of them: Charles, Danielle and Sherry, Nora and he had come together at Charles's garage this one last time before the Town Hall Meeting.

"I'm so happy we could all make it today," he said. "We will need to support each other in the coming days. This could be a dangerous undertaking, and I want to make sure that each of you understands the graveness of holding a meeting that may offend members of The Coalition. I'm not sure how they will respond."

Charles turned his eyes to his old friend and then glanced around the room to get everybody's attention. "We have been told that Wolfgang Grimm, Sam Chong, Melody Lloyd and Tom Alexander will attend. I was a bit surprised at that but, with any luck they're hoping to solve some issues as well."

"I can't see them wanting to do anything to help anybody other than themselves," Danielle snorted. Sherry elbowed her and frowned.

"I understand your distrust entirely," said Nora. "I've been wondering why they would want to come as well, unless it is self-serving." She left her chair and went to the corner to grab a coffee. "Anybody else want some?"

There was no response from anyone so she returned to her chair holding the coffee cup in both hands. "Galen, are you saying we need to be afraid for our safety because of this?"

"I'm not really sure," Galen answered. "We know we're taking a chance by stepping on some very sensitive, yet very powerful toes. I'm really not sure what they're capable of or how far they would go to stop us."

Charles leaned back in his chair and crossed his arms across his chest. "We are not doing anything wrong. We are simply having a discussion with other people about what's going on in our community and, for that matter, around the country. We're only going to pass on information and people can do with that what they wish. We may even learn some things we are currently unaware of."

Sherry looked over at Danielle, then up at Galen. "I must say I'm quite afraid of this. I've never done anything other than what I was told my entire life."

"You're not alone in that, Sherry," Galen said. "That's the story for the vast majority of Canadians. We have been turned into a country of slaves by believing, first, that our governments rule us instead of us ruling governments, and second, that when The Coalition took over we had to blindly follow the lead of those puppets that they controlled. We've reached a point of critical mass where if we don't do something now there will be no chance of recovery."

"The lives of people are at stake," said Nora. "The incidence of poisonings, as well as conditions such as autism and diseases like cancer are rising exponentially. The hospital and doctors' offices are being inundated with new cases on a regular basis."

The five of them were startled when they heard a vehicle pull up in the yard. Charles ran to the door while Danielle leaped to the window. Danielle's heart pounded as the old Chevy pickup slid to a halt, the dust behind it continuing to surround it. She watched as a middle-aged man stepped out of the vehicle followed abruptly by a husky-shepherd cross dog. The man checked around the yard.

"It's a man and a dog," she whispered hoarsely across the room to Charles. "He's just standing there looking around."

Nora rushed to the window and peered out. She then hurried to the door, opened it and stepped out into the yard. "Landon!" she called. "I'm so glad you could come. It is so nice to see you. Come. Come inside and meet everyone."

Landon followed her into the garage with Bob closely at his heels. As he stepped over the threshold he stopped and caught the eyes of the others in the room, one at a time. The dog stood by his side panting lightly with his tail wagging.

Nora made the introductions to everybody and told them briefly of the chat that she and Landon had had by the river; how she had let him know about their meetings. She included the story of Keira's death and Landon's attempt to save her.

When she finished, Landon stood fully erect, looking around at everyone. "As Nora told you, I have been doing my best to not get tangled up in anything that involves government, The Coalition, or anything else that included people for that matter. Watching what happened to that little girl has changed my mind. I have learnt things, and have seen things that should never be happening anywhere. So, if there's something I can do to help, you only have to let me know."

Sherry slid off her chair and called to Bob. She went down on one knee and held out her hand. Bob trotted to her to receive the attention she was offering. She petted his head and then wrapped her arms around his neck and gave him a hug. Her eyes moved up to Landon.

"He's beautiful." Her eyes surveyed the others. "If Nora invited him then he's more than welcome as far as I'm concerned."

Galen looked over at Charles who nodded in return. "You are welcome here, Landon. We have much to do and much to learn. The more hands available to do the work, the better it will be."

Charles returned to the table and handed Landon one of the flyers for the Town Hall Meeting. "I trust you've heard of this?"

"Yes. It was when I saw these flyers plastered all over town that I decided that I had to come and join in your effort. I'm not sure what I have to offer but you're welcome to whatever I have."

The next hour was spent bringing Landon up to date on the preparations that had already been made and providing him with the information that the other five possessed. He learnt that this small group had come together to see what they could do about protecting what was left of Yukon and her people. They told him that it would be necessary to have others join in their efforts to create a movement before they could create change. The hope was that if the movement was successful in the small territory, it could spread across the country. They explained the dangers to him and then asked if he was still interested in joining them.

"It sounds a lot more interesting than what I've been doing for a long time," he said. "I'm in."

Charles shook Landon's hand as he considered his eyes. "I'm sure we will all work well together." The others, including Galen, gave both Landon and Bob welcoming hugs.

Galen broke the reverie by asking Landon what he'd meant when he'd said he had 'learnt things and seen things' that helped with his decision to want to make change.

Landon pulled a sixth chair up to the table and invited the others to sit with him.

"For starters," he said. "There is a mine less than 20 kilometres from Whitehorse that…"

Chapter 11

The room was ready. Fifty chairs were placed in rows facing a single table with two chairs that stood at the front. They were laid out covering the entire floor from wall to wall with the exception of an aisle in the middle. At the back of the room, double doors afforded entry with an emergency exit in the corner at the front of the room. The microphone stand and mic were centred in the aisle between the front rows of chairs.

Charles busied himself making sure the chairs were in straight lines, and then paced back and forth across the front of the room. Galen sat at the table arranging and re-arranging the several stacks of paper in front of him.

"I sure hope we get some people coming out for this," said Charles. "Between the flyers and word-of-mouth, everybody must know about it by now."

Galen raised one eyebrow and quietly said, "We will get those who are supposed to be here. We have no control of how many people will show up."

A bustle of activity at the entrance caught their attention. They turned to see Danielle and Sherry come in. Sherry skipped toward the front of the room to give the two men a hug while Danielle walked in slowly, her demeanour as serious as ever.

"I see everything is ready for people to come," Sherry said as she took in the room. She noticed the counter at the back of the room and saw that it was fully stocked with bottles of water and glasses. "Well, at least no one will get a dry throat," she giggled.

Galen smiled back at her and turned toward Danielle. "How are you doing, Danielle?" he asked. "You look like you are ready to go into battle."

"Isn't that exactly what we're doing?"

"In a way, I suppose it is," he said. "Ideally though, today will only be an information session and other events can spin off of this one. I'm really not expecting too many people to come and I expect it will be a rather short meeting. But it's a beginning."

Danielle took Sherry's hand as they moved to the front row and chose their seats close to the centre aisle.

Only a few people had arrived by about 20 minutes before the meeting was to begin. Galen and Landon smiled at them in welcome but received little in response. Billy Thorsen was among them, stepping up and accosting others, obviously intoxicated. Charles glanced at his watch and continued pacing.

A short time later, Vice-President Chong and his entourage arrived. They moved directly to the front of the room and took seats in the front row on the side of the aisle opposite Danielle and Sherry. Grimm, Chong, Lloyd and Alexander sat motionless and unspeaking. Mahalia turned every few moments to see behind them. Every couple of minutes, Sherry leaned forward to see what they were doing and then quickly sat back in her chair.

At 6:55 p.m. Galen raised his head to see a room that was void of people with the exception of those few who had arrived earlier. He turned to Charles. "This is even fewer than I thought. Even some of our group are missing. Any idea where Nora and Landon are?"

"I haven't heard from them, I was expecting them to be here," said Charles as he raised his watch into view. The digits rolled over, reading 7:00 p.m. He pursed his lips, then raised his head and began to speak.

"Welcome, everyone," he said, his eyes fastened on the back of the room first and allowing his gaze to come to those sitting in the front. His voice echoed through the emptiness of the room. "I'm glad you could—"

A commotion at the door interrupted him. Everyone in the room turned to watch as large numbers of people flooded through the opening and began taking seats. The room began to fill from the back to the front.

Relief was evident on both men when they saw Nora arrive and take a seat on their left, against the wall. A moment later, Landon, with Bob beside him, strode through the door with a young First Nations man and an even younger-appearing blond woman. The youthful pair moved to the side of the room on Charles's right and settled into a couple of chairs. The woman pulled a recorder out of her backpack, nestled a notebook on her lap and sat back to inspect the room. Her companion slowly took in the scene. Landon carried a chair to the back corner opposite the doors and then sat down with the chair tipped back as he leaned against the wall. Bob lay on the floor beside him.

Galen smiled and motioned for Charles to sit beside him. As Charles lowered himself into the chair he leaned his ear toward Galen. "It appears that we're all here," said Galen. "And so many people have come. This is wonderful."

Sherry had been standing and searching through the crowd. She let out a little squeal, clapped her hands and sat down beside Danielle. "He's here! He came! I'm so excited. He's here!"

"Who?" asked Danielle.

117

"Gérard. Remember? Gérard Ponthieux, the photographer we met on the hike to The Tors. I sent him an invitation, and he came!"

Danielle frowned and turned in her seat so she could see where Sherry had been watching. At first she couldn't see anyone in particular through the mass of faces but then she saw it, the same gray toque that had introduced his arrival in the mountains. She turned, sat back in her seat, and squeezed Sherry's hand. Landon got up and quietly closed the doors to the room.

Charles rose from his chair and addressed the audience. "Welcome, everyone," he repeated. "It's so very wonderful to see you all here. My name is Charles Fleming. The gentleman seated to my right is Galen Hamel. We're here tonight to exchange information on some subjects that we believe are very important to all of us. This is a Town Hall Meeting so it will be rather informal, although we will ask that only one person speak at a time. Galen will coordinate the speakers. I'll turn it over to him now."

Galen sat upright in his chair and observed the entire room. The three men in their pin-stripes and the woman in the gray pant suit sitting in the front row with the Mulatto woman in the red dress stood out in the crowd of casually dressed people that had arrived for the meeting.

"You had us concerned for a few minutes," he chuckled. "I was beginning to think that no one would come."

"There was some guys in the parking lot telling everyone the meeting had been moved to the multiplex," shouted a woman from the middle of the crowd.

"Yeah, what the hell was that all about?" yelled a man to the left.

"Gentlemen, ladies." Galen's voice was loud enough to be heard, but gentle in its approach. "We don't know anything about that, but be that as it may, we are very happy that you came back."

I can't believe this is still going on after all these years, Galen thought. He recalled elections from decades prior when people were intentionally sent to the wrong place to vote.

He was about to continue when the doors burst inward and eight uniformed militia members stomped into the room. Director Poste was accompanied by his usual two bodyguards, but this time he had five more with him. A murmur went up in the crowd as people nudged each other, each casting a furtive glance to the back of the room.

Poste motioned for the militia to spread out across the rear of the room. He stood in the middle with his arms crossed and his legs spread. He stared defiantly toward the two men at the table.

"Do you have a permit for this gathering?" he demanded. "If you don't have one I'm going to stop this meeting right now and arrest you both." He sneered around the room as he stepped forward, the other members of the militia moving in behind him.

"Actually, yes, we do," Galen said as he held up a sheet of paper.

Poste stopped dead in his tracks about 3 metres up the centre aisle and glanced around at the crowd. He motioned his men back. "Okay, then," he growled through pursed lips. "Get on with it."

Galen smiled at him and then cleared his throat.

"We're here to discuss several issues," he began. "Some of these include questions such as what happened that made it necessary for us to have to buy water only

119

from approved sources? We have been told that it's unsafe to grow our own food so we are not allowed to do that either. Why is that? There are questions around mining regulations, as well as oil and gas regulations that affect each of you, individually. And the biggest question of all is the question of whether The Coalition is actually benefiting you, the people, or strictly itself. We are not here to voice an opinion one way or the other. We are here only to impart information and to gather your concerns, beliefs, and information."

Charles stood up behind the table and slowly opened a folder of papers in front of him.

"Let's begin with a discussion on hydraulic fracturing," he said. "Fracking is a permitted use for foreign companies because of *The Agreement*. For those of you who are too young or don't remember how *The Agreement* came to be, I'll give you a brief history.

"There was an agreement entered into by Canada and China in 2012, a *Foreign Investment Promotion and Protection Agreement,* or *FIPPA* for short. It was intended to entice foreign investors to set up shop in Canada. Part of *The Agreement* was that if any level of government introduced legislation that affected the profits of one of the companies, the corporations could then sue the Government of Canada or other level. One of the first agreements under this act was with Chinese interests. The reality is that *The Agreement* was done on behalf of companies who were owned by the Chinese state. That agreement set a precedent for other agreements with other foreign nationals. As more companies became involved, they formed a conglomerate named The Coalition for Citizens' Benefit. That coalition began running the country through the governments as a result of the judgements of arbitrators that bankrupted the country. They don't even bother to hide the fact that The Coalition runs the governments any longer."

He peered around and waited for the buzz in the room to lessen before he continued. Chong's eyes narrowed as he glared toward Charles and Galen.

"Another downside to the *FIPPA* agreements was that, in effect, they allowed foreign-owned companies to conduct exploration, mining, and oil and gas extraction in Canada without being bound by the safety, environmental and employment standards that had been set for native Canadians. That allowed them to use methods that were considered environmentally unsafe and to use employees that were not from Canada and who were not protected by Canadian wage rates or health coverage."

Charles turned to Galen. "Galen will now lead a short discussion on hydraulic fracturing, commonly known as 'fracking.'"

Charles sat in his chair as Galen looked up from the documents in front of him and turned his eyes from one side of the room to the other.

"Let's start with the positive points of fracking," Galen began. "The argument in favour of fracking is that it is more economical than traditional methods of extracting oil and gas."

"Yeah! So that creates more jobs and a stronger economy!" shouted a voice from the crowd. "What the hell's wrong with that?"

Charles rose from his chair again and interrupted.

"Before we go on, let me remind you all that this is a Town Hall Meeting and there will be opportunity for you to come to the mic to have your say," he said as he pointed toward the microphone stand between the audience and the front table. He nodded at Galen and sat down.

Galen continued. "Now, as I was saying, fracking can be a very efficient and economical way of getting at oil and gas resources. However, its use creates some environmental and health concerns. Some environmental impacts that have been recorded in the areas where fracturing has been used include the contamination of groundwater, the release of gases and hydraulic fracturing chemicals to the surface of the earth and the resultant damage to air quality in the area. In some areas, the soil around the hydraulic fracturing has been contaminated by spills from the work area. In numerous locations throughout North America, fracking has caused the earth's plates to shift, resulting in earthquakes that have disturbed and polluted entire watersheds.

"Why, right along the Alaska Highway back in 2012, areas where fracking was used extensively had problems with water purity...Pink Mountain comes to mind. No studies were ever done to connect the two, but it seems suspect. That same year, a number of ravens were found either dead or dying up and down the highway—"

A man deep in the crowd to their left jumped up from his chair. "Everything seems to be working just fine here though. There's an old saying, 'If it ain't broke don't fix it.' So why are you trying to fix it?"

"There is much truth in that old proverb, my friend," said Galen. "However, I expect we will learn tonight that things are beyond being 'broke'. They have been destroyed. If you have some data on fracking to the contrary we would be happy to see it." Galen waited a few seconds. "Nothing? You can sit down again."

He turned and nodded to Charles to take over. Charles rose, shuffled the sheets of paper and continued.

"Another issue we would like to discuss is mining regulations. There is evidence that companies who are not adhering to the existing regulations are not taking the necessary precautions when they are extracting minerals and are causing irreversible harm to the environment around their operations."

Melody Lloyd glared at the two men facing her. She slid forward on her chair and leaned across Mahalia's lap. Reaching past Grimm, she poked Chong's leg to get his attention. "How long are you going to let this go on?" she breathed. "You need to put a stop to it now."

Chong glanced down at her poking fingers and turned to her. "Don't ever touch me again," he growled. "I will decide if and when this needs to stop." With a jerk of his head he indicated the militia at the back of the room. "We have things under control so sit back and say nothing."

She sat back in her chair, then turned and glared at Alexander. He turned to her with one eyebrow raised, and slowly turned to look back toward the front of the room. She expected him to support her more than he seemed capable of. Perhaps she had made an error in hiring him.

Charles continued with his prepared speech.

"The next concern that has been raised that we might want to discuss tonight is the question of whether it is safe to grow your own food or not. As you all know, The Coalition has decreed that you can only use water that was provided by a source that has been approved by them. That raises the question as to why. Is it to ensure our safety? Or is it to increase corporate profits? They tell us that the groundwater is no longer safe for our use. Is that true? And if so, what caused it to be so polluted? What noxious substances have been introduced and by whom?"

Charles sat in his chair and turned to Galen, tapping him on the shoulder. Galen was already starting to look a bit tired, but after taking a deep breath he began.

"As we mentioned earlier, there is also the question of whether The Coalition is truly benefiting the people or simply ensuring its own profits. After all, it is companies controlled by The Coalition who are benefiting the most by having free rein on what they do in Canada. Do any of you have something to say on any of these topics?" he asked.

A man who had been sitting beside a woman and two young children stood and made his way to the front. He reached forward with one quivering hand and rested it on the mic.

"I think you're only having this meeting to cause trouble," his voice wavered. "We listen to the news all the time so I know that none of the problems you are talking about have anything to do with mining or oil and gas. This is crap that tree huggers spout off to try and blame The Coalition for everything. None of it is true. The other thing is that we have people in government that represent us so we know we're being looked after. After all, that's the public servants' job." He turned to go back to his chair, then hesitated and his lips tightened when he saw his wife and two kids. He turned again to go back to the microphone.

"We know exactly what's going on because people from the government explained it to us personally after our little boy died from cyanide poisoning he got from drinking water from a well. They explained that we were at fault because they had told us that we were only to drink water from approved sources and we had let him drink from our well. Since then, they have capped off all the wells in the area so it doesn't happen again. Isn't that proof that they're doing the best thing for us?" He turned again, hung his head and ambled back to his chair.

Gwen Doyle was incensed. She leaped out of her chair and yelled from the other side of the room.

"Who the hell do you think owns the news?" she shouted as she pushed her way through the row of chairs toward the mic stand. When she reached it she grabbed the mic and whirled around staring straight into the man's eyes.

"The same fucking corporations that form The Coalition and are running our country through these dummy governments own all the news outlets, you idiot! We haven't heard an honest piece of news since they disbanded CBC after the last election over 20 years ago. Your baby died because they poisoned him. I know because our little girl is gone because of them too!"

"Gwen!" shouted Paddy from his chair beside where she'd been sitting. He was startled by her sudden, unexpected outburst. "Come back and sit down, please. You can't blame The Coalition for everything. We were told that it was a freak happening and—"

"YOU SHUT THE FUCK UP!" Gwen screamed across the room at him. "Just shut the fuck up! Our little girl is dead and you don't give a shit who caused it? So, shut the fuck up." She stopped and glared around the room with tears streaming down her face. "Don't let them keep doing this. Don't let them keep lying to us. They're not doing any of you any favours."

She stood still for a moment and then, with a deep breath, turned and marched down the aisle with her shoulders back and her head held high. She kept her eyes straight ahead as she moved toward the door. At the back of the room she found herself face to face with a scowling Poste. She stopped, her face only centimetres from his, and snarled. Landon stood up at the back of the room while several men in the audience began to rise from their chairs and turn toward the unfolding confrontation. Poste glanced around the room, then stepped aside to let her pass. She stormed past him, pulling both doors open on her way through. They swung shut behind her.

Silence enveloped the room.

After allowing a couple of moments to pass, Galen called the meeting back to order.

"Some of you may remember," he began, "that back in 2012 the city of Whitehorse was using an exorbitant amount of chlorine and other purifiers in the water. The reason given at that time was that it was due to natural bacteria and impurities. However, it turned out that the substances in the water were caused by some unauthorized fracking. Documents now indicate that the practice was being ignored by the very government departments that were supposed to be enforcing a moratorium that was in place at the time."

Grimm, Chong, Lloyd and Alexander began to squirm in their chairs. Mahalia sat calmly facing the two men at the table in front of her. Galen extended an invitation to see if anyone else wanted to add to the discussion.

Nora made her way toward the microphone and spoke while facing Charles and Galen.

"I'd like to add to the comments about the public servants," she said as she faced the front table. "I'm a nurse so I qualify as one of those employees. Remember that, beginning in 2011, the numbers of public servants have been decimated by cutbacks and layoffs. There is little to no service from any level of government these days. Those employees who are left have become the pseudo-enforcers of the rules pertaining to water, mines, and oil and gas. They are compliant with the demands of their employer simply to keep their jobs. Canadians, most of us in this room, have remained apathetic and unwilling to step outside our perceived comfort/safety zone of government care. Our assessment of the situation has been pure folly."

She stopped, and then walked around the mic stand to face the audience.

"We haven't had any elections since Martial Law was declared back in 2018. The government that arose from that has created rules and laws designed to denigrate us, the citizens of Canada, to bring us to compliance. Our world has become a living oligarchy where everything that is done must be for the benefit of The Coalition. The government is only a pretense, a way to hold Canadians at ransom under *The Agreement*."

Chong leaped out of his chair and thrust a shaking finger in Nora's direction.

"Your talk borders on treason," he berated. "At the very least it could be seen as incitement to riot." He turned to the back of the room and glowered at Poste. "Do something! Put a stop to this!" he roared.

Poste jumped in fright, and then motioned for the militia to follow him up the aisle to where Nora stood her ground. The crowd rose, then closed in behind Poste as he made his way to the front; their action preventing the other militia members from following him. As Poste reached the front of the room, Galen moved around the table and stood between him and Nora.

"Get out of the way, old man," Poste growled.

Galen continued to stand, quietly and peacefully between them. Poste felt the energy of the crowd getting higher and turning against him. Galen challenged him.

"What do you intend to do, arrest me? Beat me?"

Poste stepped toward Galen until only mere centimetres separated them. Galen held his head high, his eyes trained on the back of the room, refusing to be drawn into a showdown. Poste whirled around to order the militia to step in and realized that he was alone—it was only him, Galen, and the large crowd. He turned back to Galen. "You're gonna pay for this, you old fucker."

Galen allowed his view to drop to meet Poste's eyes.

"You are a funny little man, aren't you?" he said in a barely audible tone so only Poste would hear.

Poste turned, put his head down and slumped toward the crowd. An opening barely wide enough for him to enter appeared and then closed behind him as he made his way to the back of the room. When he was surrounded by the militia, he spun on his heel toward the gathering.

He was about to give the order to arrest Galen when the sound of metal sliding against metal and a distinct double-click sent a shiver up his spine. To his right, Landon stood with his rifle in both hands after racking a round into the chamber. A glint of white caused him to glance down as Bob's curled lips exposed his massive canine teeth. Poste turned on shaking knees and pushed the militia man beside him out of his way. He stomped toward the exit with the uniformed men falling in line behind him. He stopped at the doorway.

"This is not over, you bastards," he growled, then turned and stormed through the doors.

The audience returned to their seats. Grimm, Chong, Lloyd and Alexander sat motionless for a moment, then quickly moved out of their chairs and left the building through the corner exit at the front of the room. Mahalia's form-fitted red gown was seen following at a leisurely pace.

Galen glanced at the scattered array of papers on the table, and then raised his eyes to the crowd.

"My friends, I ask you to think long and hard about what you've heard and seen here tonight. Consider what is going on in your lives, in your community and in your country. What do you want to do for yourselves, your families and your community? Will you stand up for what is right? Will you speak in defence of your neighbour? Think about this quote from Martin Luther King Jr. 'In the end we will remember not the words of our enemies...but the silence of our friends'."

With that, he called the meeting to a close.

The murmur in the room slowly rose to a crescendo of voices. Some were still arguing the merits of The Coalition while others, the majority, were discussing how their lives had changed since the advent of the corporate-run governments, and how it seemed that everything they did was only for the benefit of The Coalition for Citizens' Benefit. They were questioning who was responsible for the noxious materials that had found their way into the water tables. Many were muttering about putting an end to the reign of their corporate masters.

The deliberations continued as the room emptied.

Nora, Landon, Stone and Kirsten moved to the front of the room and surrounded the two men at the head table. Danielle and Sherry quickly joined them. Bob sat between the first two rows, his gaze fixed firmly on the doors at the back of the hall.

"Great meeting," said Stone. "It really got people thinking."

Kirsten came around the table and leaned over and hugged Galen. "I have so much great material for an article. If I can get it published it'll help get more people thinking about standing up for themselves. Hopefully it will go national."

She stepped over to hug Charles. "Thank you so much for having the nerve to do this."

"That could've turned really ugly," said Landon. "We're lucky that Poste and his goons walked away instead of retaliating."

He moved closer to Galen who was sitting contentedly in his chair. "That took a lot of nerve, standing up to Poste the way you did. How did you know he wouldn't try and take you down?"

"He's little more than a bully. And I was trusting in the truth that bullies are truly cowards at heart. Fortunately, like most of his ilk, he turned and ran as soon as the going got a little tough. I am really glad it went that way." The other five nodded in agreement.

Charles reached over and grasped Galen's arm gently. "It's a good thing you thought of getting a permit for this. I didn't even know we needed one."

Galen reached into the folder in front of him and drew out the permit that he had waved at Poste from across the room. He turned it over and laid it on the table. The others burst into laughter. He had merely shown the letterhead from his property tax bill.

"There's much to do now," Galen said. "They'll not be forgetting what happened here tonight, so any of us they believe are connected with this meeting will not be safe. They could be coming for us at any time."

Landon grinned wryly. "Well, like the old saying goes, 'there's nothing like hanging at dawn to focus the mind.'"

Chapter 12

"I want those two arrested," Chong growled as they scuttled out of the High Country Inn meeting room. "I want them in jail. Where the hell did Poste go? I told him to do something—and he did nothing except run."

Mahalia sat between Grimm and Chong on one side of the limo while Lloyd and Alexander took the other for the short ride to Grimm's Main Street office. When they entered the leather-upholstered elevator on the way to the third floor, Grimm stepped in front of Chong, facing him.

"I suggest that you be very careful how you deal with them," he said. "It would be too easy to make a martyr out of an old man. I think it's important to recognize that neither of them voiced any opinion, only facts. All they did was to remind people of facts."

The elevator opened and they paused in the hallway while Mahalia unlocked the office doors. They strode through the outer office into Grimm's inner sanctum, leaving Mahalia behind. Grimm went directly to the liquor cabinet and slid the glass doors open. He pulled out a bottle of single malt scotch.

"Anybody else want one?" he asked. Lloyd and Alexander hustled to the bar and accepted the amber liquid. Chong paced back and forth, his face burning.

"If we let them get away with that it will encourage more rabble-rousers," he droned.

Lloyd winced as she threw back the scotch. After watching her, Alexander sniffed the rim of his glass tentatively and then took a very small sip. He was surprised to feel it burn all the way down his gullet. He frowned incredulously as he looked over at his boss who, by then, had recovered from the effects of swallowing the powerful fluid and was requesting another.

"Are you okay, Melody?" he asked.

"I've never been better," she snapped back at him. "What do you think? Our company could be held responsible for causing the death of that little girl. We could be found guilty of polluting a water system that people are using, dammit. Yeah, sure, I'm doing just fine."

You did authorize it, you stupid bitch, he thought. *Now we have to find a way out.*

Alexander turned to Chong. "What are you going to do about this? We need to keep the attention away from our mine. Maybe spread the word that those who held the Town Hall Meeting are no more than environmental extremists; that what they are saying is only propaganda."

Grimm moved in behind his desk and settled into his large overstuffed chair. He leaned back and sipped his scotch.

"As I said before, if you go after those two you will turn them into martyrs and the public will distrust anything you do after that." He watched as Chong became more agitated, pacing faster and clenching and unclenching his fists. "Vice-President Chong, maybe you should have a drink. It might help to settle your nerves," he persuaded.

"Don't tell me what I should have," Chong sputtered. "We will find a way to deal with them. Nobody makes a fool out of me."

Lloyd's eyes snapped to Chong. "Maybe there's a perfect solution," she said. "If something were to just 'happen' to them we couldn't be blamed and it may very well stop this whole bout of foolishness." She turned to Alexander. "Do you know anybody that can look after this? It's time you made yourself useful."

Alexander kept his head down and hesitantly turned his eyes toward her. It was very difficult for him to deal with her under pressure, especially when she was angry—it was too much like dealing with his mother.

"I agree with Wolfgang," he croaked. "I think we need to lay low for a good period of time now to make sure that if anything were to happen to them it won't be connected to us. We need to move slowly, and take our time to make sure this is done right." Alexander didn't like the idea of being a part of her suggested plan.

Grimm stepped out of his chair and walked around his desk to the other three. He moved in and put his face close to Alexander's.

"What do you mean, you agree with me?" he said hoarsely. "I never said anything about anything happening to them." He turned to the others, interfering with Chong's persistent walking. "I don't have any problem enforcing rules, regulations and laws but I will have no part of hurting people. My job is to make sure that The Capitol is properly represented and that people understand how The Coalition makes their lives better. I am not going to be part of causing harm to anyone."

He turned back to his chair and sat in front of his drink.

Chong whirled to face him and slammed his fist on the desk. "You will do exactly as you are told!" he snarled.

The eruption caused Alexander to jump, spilling his drink as Lloyd watched him, shaking her head in disgust. She scrutinized Grimm, then Chong, then Grimm again as she pointed an accusing finger directly at him.

"You are going to have to man up," she said. "We have to do whatever is necessary to protect my company and you know it. In order for our mines and the oil and gas industry to keep the economy growing, we need to be able to do whatever has to be done to keep the investors happy. Sometimes that means getting your hands a little dirty."

She leaned over Grimm's desk to put her face closer to his. "Are you up for it or not?" she asked.

Grimm's eyes narrowed. "I will have nothing to do with anybody getting hurt," he said. "I don't want to know anything about it."

Chong turned and leaned back on the front of the desk—and found himself face to face with Alexander who had moved in behind him.

"What about your Director of Militia?" Alexander demanded. "He was incompetent during that little conflict. How are you going to deal with that?"

"I will deal with him personally," rumbled Chong. "There was no excuse for him to have run the way he did."

Chong broke eye contact with Alexander and turned to Lloyd. "If you had better security at your mine, this wouldn't have happened. Hire your own people if you have to. Obviously, the outfit that's been doing it hasn't been very successful."

"I have already done that," she retorted. "But it wasn't the break-in that caused that meeting, so don't try and lay the blame on me. We have stopped production at the mine and flushed the entire system, including the creek so that it runs clear and clean now. We'll have the Department of Health test the water so that we have proof that there is nothing wrong with the drainage from that site. We are well underway toward building our defence."

Chong's expression softened. "I wish you would have been as proactive before this problem started as you are being now," said Chong. "As soon as you can confirm that every test is completely safe, go ahead and get the Minister of Health to run the necessary examinations."

Chong stared around the room at the others. "There's nothing more to be done here. I'll call you when we need to meet again." He turned on his heel and strutted out of the office.

Grimm was incredulous. *Who gave Chong the right to control me*, he wondered? *Who did Chong think he was to decide that there was no more to discuss?*

On the other side of the door, Mahalia had pulled her ear from the door and jumped back quickly to sit at her desk. She watched as Chong stormed through the outer office, pushing his way through the door and then, after stabbing at the call button several times, stepped into the elevator. *This man will be Wolfgang's undoing*, she thought. *He needs to be stopped.*

I don't care what anybody says, Chong thought. *I'm not going to let them get away with it.* When he got to the street he pulled out his cell phone and pressed the number two, holding it down until the speed dial made the connection.

"Hello? Poste here."

"This is Chong. I have some work for you to do. And you better be successful with this or there'll be hell to pay."

After everyone left, Mahalia went through the office cleaning glasses and straightening up the room, all the while considering if Chong was a menace. She went back to her desk and sat looking at the telephone. After waiting a moment, she reached forward and pulled the phone book from the desk drawer. She flipped through the pages to the "M's" and then slid her finger down the left side of the page until a name was highlighted above her immaculately manicured nail.

Landon McGuire—she reached for the receiver.

Kirsten jumped as her daydream was abruptly interrupted when the toaster popped. She left the table and moved to the counter and began spreading butter on the sprouted multi-grain slices. Her head turned when she heard the water in the shower turn off and she watched as the bathroom door opened. Stone walked into the kitchen with a towel wrapped around his waist.

"Good morning, lovely lady," he said as he grinned at her. "Would you like me to make some coffee?"

"Already done. Pour one for me while you're at it, please. I put some toast in for you."

He reached into the 70's vintage cupboards and withdrew two heavy porcelain mugs. As he poured the hot, dark fluid, his eyes turned to Kirsten. She had stopped slathering butter on a piece of toast and stood with her eyes fixed on it.

"Are you still thinking about the town hall meeting...or waiting for a response from the editor?" he asked.

Kirsten had been lost in thought about the article she'd sent to *Canadiana*, the largest national magazine in Canada. She stood erect and turned her head back to him. "Yes. I sent that piece to them a week ago. I know it's far too soon to expect any kind of response, but I can't seem to get it out of my mind." She dropped two more slices into the toaster and carried the others to the old wooden table, setting them beside several jars of jams and honeys.

"What would happen if you followed up by contacting them? I've done that a few times when I was submitting papers to environmental science organizations. If nothing else, it helped me stop thinking about it for a few days."

Stone brought the two steaming mugs to the table and sat in one of the two straight-backed chairs.

Kirsten's hand stopped midway toward bringing a piece of toast to her mouth. "I don't know. I've never done that. I've always waited for a response." The toast continued its journey and she sat chewing, looking straight ahead, her eyes unfocused.

The new batch of toast jumped up and Stone went to the counter to retrieve them. He grabbed a small plate and the butter and returned to the table.

"I think it would be useful for you to give the editor a call. It's a great piece of investigative journalism, something that has been lacking for a long time. I don't think you can do any harm. They're either going to accept it or they're not."

"Maybe you're right. At least it'd be better than sitting here with it eating away at me." She raised the thick white mug to her lips, sipping hot coffee carefully. "I'll do that right after breakfast."

"And if that doesn't take your mind off of it, maybe I can think of something that will." Stone winked at her.

She slapped playfully at his hand. "That did seem to help for a while," she giggled.

After breakfast, Kirsten went to the telephone and dialled the number for the editor of *Canadiana*. Stone went to the bedroom to get dressed.

By the time Stone returned to the kitchen, Kirsten was already at the table nursing her coffee. He sat across from her at the small, round table top.

"That was fast. I take it she wasn't in?"

Kirsten raised the mug with both hands and sipped her coffee again. "She was there. The conversation was quite short. As soon as she realized she was talking to me she explained that her employers simply would not allow her to publish an article that put The Coalition in a bad light. But she did give me something else." Her eyes sparkled as she observed Stone.

He waited as she smiled silently at him. "And...what was that?" he asked when he couldn't wait any longer.

"She gave me the name of a publication that is run by a non-profit organization and asked me if it would be okay to forward my transcript to them. Of course, I said she could."

The *Current Chronicle* was a new, nation-wide magazine that was not funded in any way by government or corporations. Their advertisers were small mom-and-pop businesses and individuals. The balance of their income was from subscriptions.

"Any idea when you can expect to hear from them?"

"No idea, but I do have their phone number."

She didn't have to wait long. Two days later, she received a call from the editor of the *Current Chronicle* asking for verification on some of the statements she'd made. Her article had made reference to increases in conditions such as autism as well as diseases, with cancer being a prime example. She referred them to the data from Autism Awareness Canada that showed that the prevalence of autism in Canada had risen from one in 88 in 2012 to closer to one in 50 by 2035. Similar statistics from the National Cancer Society showed a substantial increase in the number of people developing cancer. It had risen from two people in five in 2011 to closer to four in five by 2034.

She substantiated that the federal government and The Coalition had supported studies and research into mitigating illnesses and conditions but none into seeking the initial cause of the increases. One case in point was the study done on stem cell research to ameliorate the impact of autism that began in 2012, and proved to be somewhat successful by 2015. They refused to fund or allow studies toward finding and eradicating the causes. The Coalition had gone as far as adding to existing legislation, effectively muzzling scientists and making it a criminal offence for those scientists to speak publicly on their findings.

Kirsten's protected source had provided the necessary verification on the increased numbers of oil and gas companies using fracking throughout southern Yukon, complete with dates and locations. The timing of these increases coincided with the contamination of both the watersheds and the water table, making it unsafe for the public to use water from anywhere natural and making it necessary to use only what The Coalition provided. The same source had also provided information on mining activity—including one mine very close to Whitehorse.

She was able to provide all the substantiation they needed.

Another day passed and the phone rang again. Kirsten rushed to answer it. Stone watched as she stood passively listening to the voice on the other end before he heard her say a quiet, "Thank you," and hang up.

She turned to him as her eyes welled up.

"They're going to publish it! It's going to hit the newsstands next week!" She began jumping up and down as she held the phone close to her chest. In the midst of her excitement she stopped still, and turned to Stone. "I wonder what will happen now?"

He moved to her and enveloped her in his arms; her head leaned on his shoulder.

"I imagine there's going to be some very upset people when it gets read," he said softly. "I think for the time being it's best that you don't go out alone and that when you do, you stay in public places. But more importantly, congratulations on a job well done." He kissed the top of her head and pulled her closer.

Chapter 13

Sherry flitted around the single floor bungalow at the foot of Grove Street where she and Danielle had made their home for nine years. She dusted all the furniture in the living room and then wiped down all the counters and tabletops in the dining area and kitchen. The carpets were vacuumed and the floors mopped while cookies baked in the oven. Everything was to be perfect when Gérard arrived.

She checked the kitchen clock when she heard the crunching of tires on the gravel in the driveway: 5:15 p.m. *That will be Danielle*, she thought, *just like clockwork—home every day at exactly the same time.* She rushed to the front door to greet her.

She pulled the door open—and was at first dumbstruck, then alarmed. Two uniformed militia officers stood on the doorstep. The taller of the two stepped past her and walked in the house, uninvited.

"Are you here alone?" he asked.

Sherry said nothing as she peered past them, through the door, searching for an avenue of escape.

"I asked you a question," he snapped. "When I ask you a question I expect to get an answer. Are you here alone?"

She dashed for the open door but the second intruder caught her by the arm. She screamed as she saw Danielle's Ford Focus turn into the driveway and pull up beside the huge Dodge sedan with tinted windows.

"What are you doing?" Danielle yelled as she leaped from her car. "Let go of her!" She ran from the car to the front porch. Sherry was still screaming, attracting the attention of neighbours on both sides of the street.

Danielle grabbed the smaller man's arm and yanked it away from Sherry. The trench-coated man inside the house hurried back out onto the porch. He raised his hand to strike at Danielle.

"Hey! What the hell are you doing?" yelled the man from the yard of the house beside them. More voices joined from the other homes and people started moving toward the Frasers' bungalow.

"This is none of your affair," said the taller of the two militia men. He waved them off with a flurry from his hand. "Go home and stay there."

"Who are you? Why are you here?" asked Danielle. "What do you want from us? Who sent you?"

The smaller of the two militia men contemplated the neighbours that had mustered in the yard. He saw an old Jeep four-wheel drive pull into the yard and come to a sliding halt behind Danielle's car. The door opened and a man stepped out. The militia man remembered seeing the large man in the gray toque before. He wondered what Gérard Ponthieux would be doing at this house. He signalled to his partner to back off.

"We're simply going around to check on those that we know were at the Town Hall Meeting the other night— to make sure that everyone is okay," the smaller man lied with a forced smile. "We didn't mean to scare you, ma'am. I see that all is well here so we'll be on our way." He jerked his head toward the driveway to signal to his cohort to follow him to the car.

The two men moved cautiously through the gathering crowd, skirting the man in the gray toque to get to their vehicle; each of them holding their coat back with one hand holding the handle of a nightstick.

"We'll be back to check up on you," said the smaller man as he got in to the driver seat.

Gérard took a step toward the car. "You better not show up here ever again," he growled.

The larger of the two men pulled the gear shift into reverse, spinning tires and throwing gravel as he backed out of the driveway. He slammed it into drive and tore up the street away from the crowd.

Danielle took a deep breath and addressed the people in their front yard. "Thank you, everyone. Thank you so much." The neighbours smiled and nodded. They chatted about the event as they returned to their homes, satisfied that their end of the street was safe.

Gérard went back to his car, retrieved a leather-bound case and then came to the porch and smiled at the two women. Sherry stretched up to give him a hug; Danielle shook his hand and patted his arm. They invited him in and as he crossed the threshold he reached up and slid the toque off his head revealing a close crop of graying hair.

"I'm so happy you could come," gushed Sherry. "I'm such a fan of your work. I'm sorry there was all that fuss when you got here."

"I don't appreciate it when people bother my friends," he said. "I'm glad I got here when I did."

Both women were touched by his mention of them being his friends. Somehow they knew he would be a great ally.

"Come into the living room," said Sherry.

"I'd be happier sitting around the kitchen table with you," smiled Gérard. "Besides, it will be easier to show you what I brought if we have a table."

Sherry rushed to a cupboard drawer to retrieve the digital memory card he had dropped in the mountains. "I better give this back to you before I forget," she tittered. Gérard accepted it with a smile.

The three of them sat and had coffee, bolstered by Sherry's freshly baked cookies, and talked for about an hour. By then, Sherry could hardly contain her excitement.

By the end of the hour, Sherry's attention was focused entirely on the hand-tooled leather case that Gérard had brought in with him. He watched as her eyes would flick between him and the case.

"Do you want to see what's in there?" he asked, teasing her.

Sherry nodded apprehensively as Danielle sat back and smiled at her. Gérard raised the briefcase to the table, unclipped the latches and opened it slowly. Inside, there were several folios of photographic prints that had been taken around Yukon. He handed them one at a time to the two women and sat patiently while they viewed each image.

"These are marvellous," said Sherry.

"Outstanding," added Danielle.

"I have one more set of photos for you to see," said Gérard. "I'll be back in a moment." He rose from the table and sauntered out the front door to his car.

When he returned he was pulling a Virtual Portable Computer out of his pocket. He went directly to the kitchen table, unfolded it and switched on the holograph screen.

"I haven't made prints of any of these because I don't want them falling into anyone's possession until I'm prepared to release them," he said. "You'll understand why when you see them."

We're going to see the very best of his photos, thought Sherry. *Photographs that are so good he's never shared them with anyone else.* She was breathless with anticipation.

Gérard reached back into the leather briefcase, slid open the zipper on the underside of the lid and took out a micro memory card. He smiled at the two women and then inserted the drive into the VPC. A moment later they were struck with a combination of awe, wonder and excitement as the images materialized on the screen.

"Is that what I think it is?" asked Danielle. "Is that a mining operation? What is so special about a mining operation?"

"It is exactly what you think it is," he said. "And much more."

He showed them through a large number of digital images, pointing out intricacies and information that may be overlooked by the everyday viewer.

"Why did you take so many pictures of a mining operation?" asked Sherry. "It's nowhere near as lovely as your other work."

"I took these because this particular mine was not doing anything to make sure that the water it used was safe to release into the watershed. These images are proof that they allowed poisonous water to escape and did nothing to try and stop it."

"But, couldn't they say that it was only a mishap that lasted for, maybe, one day, and then they fixed everything?" asked Sherry.

"They could," said Gérard, "except that these images are digitally stamped and geo-tagged so the exact date, time and physical location on the planet are a permanent part of the original file."

Danielle leaned forward and put her hand on his arm, catching his eyes. She turned back to the holograph screen.

"So, this is evidence that would be acceptable in court?"

"*Absolument*," said Gérard. "I've had my pictures used in courts before."

Danielle was mesmerized by the images on the screen. "Where is this mine?" she asked softly.

Gérard fixed his eyes directly on hers and smiled. "About 20 kilometres west of Whitehorse."

The old Sportage coughed and sputtered as Paddy brought it to a halt a block away from The People's Pub. He sat with his hands on the steering wheel, staring at the dashboard as a myriad of painful thoughts ran through his mind.

He was depressed about his inability to protect Gwen and Aaron and felt that he was only half the man he should be. Keira's death weighed heavily on him as he accepted the full blame for having taken her on the trail that fateful day. He was afraid to speak out publicly the way Gwen had for fear he would lose his job and his family would have no income. Then, on top of not being able to keep them safe, he wouldn't be a provider either. Things just kept getting worse.

The well-worn doors of the pub were only a few metres away. It had increasingly become his place of refuge, the alcohol numbing his feelings and thoughts. The arguments at home had become more frequent as his depression deepened. He had learnt that the company he worked for was responsible for the poison that killed his daughter, and every day had become a struggle to survive.

He cracked open the door of the car and slunk up the street toward his haven of oblivion. He stepped through the door to be with the same old crowd that was always there even though this was early on Wednesday afternoon.

Billy Thorsen, the perennial at the bar, was already seated at one of the small round tables in the back of the room. He waved at Paddy to join him. Although he really didn't want any company, Paddy made his way toward the table.

"Sit yourself down, Paddy," said Billy. He signalled at Star to bring a round for the table. She turned and bounced toward the bartender, her spike heels tapping on the floor.

"Damn, that is one nice looking woman," sighed Billy. "I sure wish I could get me a piece of that." Paddy glanced over at the retreating short skirt and tightly fitted top. His eyes turned back down at the table.

Billy drained the glass that was sitting in front of him, and then almost knocked it over as he set it down. "You're earlier than usual today. Did you get off work early?"

"No, I just decided to leave."

"How's that little woman of yours doing? That was quite a performance she put on at the meeting the other week. She's got a lot of spunk, that one." Billy was leaning forward trying to see Paddy's eyes.

"I suppose she's doing fine," muttered Paddy, his head hanging.

"Did ya set her straight for talking to ya like that? I'd sure be teaching her a lesson if she was my woman."

The pumps and sheer black stockings came into view in the corner of Paddy's eye as he heard the clink of glasses being set on the table. He reached in his pocket and dropped a $20 bill beside the beers. Star's garishly painted fingernails flashed before him as it disappeared onto her tray. She turned and walked away.

Paddy reached for a glass and unceremoniously drained it, then caught Star's attention. "Do me a favour and keep 'em coming," he told her. She hesitated, glanced at Paddy, and then returned to the bar to begin a long night of retrieving drinks for their table.

Paddy was no longer listening to Billy's constant prattle about the state of the world and how he was going to fix it. He lost interest in the common, everyday discussions at the drinking hole. His mind was fixated on what was going on at home with Gwen. He wanted only to see her smile again, to feel her kiss on his cheek and to know that she and Aaron were both happy and safe. He wanted to feel like a man again.

I need to make this right, he thought. *I need to find a way to show her that I'm as much a man as anybody else.*

Later in the evening he reached into his pocket to pay for the next round of drinks and came up empty. "I guess it's time for me to go," he said to Star.

She bent over and gently touched his hand. "You make sure you take a cab or walk home. You are in no condition to be driving. You look after yourself now."

Paddy nodded, then pulled himself together and walked uncertainly through the doors. He stood on the sidewalk trying to decide what to do next. He had no money to pay for a cab, and a five-kilometre walk to the Ingram subdivision was too much of a challenge to face. He turned and walked to his car.

The next thing he remembered was somebody banging on the window of the Kia. He raised his eyes to see the closely cropped head and black trench coat of a militia member. He glanced forward and saw that he was still parked on Main Street and realized that he'd simply passed out behind the wheel. He rolled down the window.

"It looks like you need a ride home, buddy," smiled the man facing him. "Come on out and we'll take you there."

"It's okay," Paddy said cautiously. "I'm fine now so I'll be able to drive myself home."

The man's expression changed from a smile to a stern glowering. "Let me rephrase that. Get out of the car. Now!" He reached down and yanked the door open.

Paddy threw himself toward the passenger door to escape but found the window was blackened by another militia uniform. He slowly slid out of the car and faced the man, keeping his eyes turned.

"You're coming with us," the man said as he grabbed at his arm and guided him toward the open door of the militia sedan. As Paddy bent over to get in the car, he was shoved and landed sprawled across the backseat. The door slammed behind him. Frantically, he examined his surroundings and saw that there was a metal screen separating the back seat from the front and that there were no handles on the inside of the back doors. He was trapped.

He was driven to an area a short distance south of the Carcross cut off, about 25 kilometres from town, where they turned off the highway onto a set of tracks leading into the bush. *Sweet Jesus*, Paddy thought, *they're going to kill me.*

The black sedan slid to a stop. "Get out," said the man who first accosted him as he pulled the back door open.

Paddy set one foot outside the car and slowly brought the rest of his body into the open. His mind was screaming. *I'm going to die. These bastards are going to beat me to death.*

The second militia man came around the car to join the first. The man who had been doing the talking pushed Paddy against the vehicle.

"You need to get better control of that bitch you're married to," he snarled. "She talks way too much and there are some people who don't appreciate it." His forearm was across Paddy's face, pressing his cheek into the glass. "Do you understand that?"

"I can't tell her what to do," Paddy sputtered. "She's her own woman and if she has something to say she's going to say it. How am I supposed to stop her?" He eyed the two men and realized that there was no way out of what was going to happen. He glared at the man holding him down. "Fuck you. Even if I could stop her, I wouldn't."

The man stepped back. Paddy started to straighten himself off the car and was met by the man's other hand as it whistled forward and slapped him. He shoved his elbow back under Paddy's chin, pressing into his throat.

"We're not *asking* you to do something, we're *telling* you. Like I said, there's some very powerful people who want her to shut up. Either you do it or we will."

Paddy struggled against the much larger man, terrified that his family was in danger.

"You go to hell! Don't you dare touch her!" he said as he grappled against the much larger man.

More pressure was applied to the elbow that was now choking him.

Paddy's hands flailed at his assailant. He pumped his legs in an attempt to kick out at the thug. The blows were ineffectual.

"Whaddya say we do a little convincin'," said the other man. "Yup, a little gentle persuasion is in order."

The first man grabbed Paddy and spun him around so he was facing the blackened-out windows. He grabbed him by the hair, pulled his head back, then forcefully pushed his face into the safety glass. Paddy could feel his nose crush against his cheek bone.

He was then thrown into the grasp of the second man who turned him to face the first while holding his arms back so he was helpless. The large man reached inside his trench coat and slid out a one-metre long nightstick. Paddy crumpled and his breath escaped him as the weapon was driven into his solar plexus. As he went down to the ground he heard a crack and felt a sharp pain as the second man drove a steel-toed boot into his ribs.

"Just do what you're told," growled the first man, "and nobody else has to get hurt. Shut that bitch up."

Paddy lay on the ground, his nose bleeding profusely, unable to catch his breath because of a broken rib. He thought of his family and the threat that these men posed for them. He swore to himself that he would find some way of getting even, some way to protect Gwen and Aaron.

"Fuck you," he managed to blurt as the two men climbed into their vehicle. They backed the car up, turned it around, and showered Paddy with dirt as they spun out of the trail.

He was left alone—alone with his hurt, frustration and anger.

I'll show them, he thought as he struggled to his feet to find his way back home. *I'll show them.*

Chapter 14

The engine of the old Chevy pickup purred as Landon brought it to a halt in the small parking area near the Rotary Centennial Bridge on the Millennium Trail. Bob whined in eager anticipation of a walk to the bench overlooking the river where they so often went. Today, however, would be different.

After making sure his Magnum was loaded and sliding one of his knives into the sheath strapped to his leg, Landon stepped away from the truck. He hesitated, thinking of a simpler time when the carrying of weapons was considered illegal, and was also unnecessary. *God. Things have changed so much in such a short time*, he thought. He started walking toward the bridge and saw that Nora was already waiting for him.

"Hi," she said smiling as he reached her. "I'm so glad you could make it." She knelt down to greet Bob as he ran up to her to receive her attention. "And how's my big boy. He's such a good boy."

She rose and faced Landon, a questioning look on her face. Then she moved forward and gave him a welcoming hug as well. Landon felt awkward as he stood still, not returning the gesture.

"I hope you don't mind meeting here," she said as she released him. "I find it better to be outdoors as much as possible." What she didn't say was that she was hesitant to bring people to her home, her refuge and place of quiet and safety.

"No, this is great," he replied. "Meeting here won't cause any suspicion either so is probably a good idea." He laughed as his attention was drawn to his dog's vigorously wagging tail. "Besides, Bob loves it on this trail."

"Actually, he's the reason I suspected you knew something about the incident at the mine," said Nora. She turned to look up the paved path.

Landon frowned. "I'm not sure I understand. I thought that when I mentioned it at the meeting at Charles's place, it was the first time anybody had heard of it."

"I'm sure it was. But don't forget I was in the emergency ward when the guards from the mine were brought in for treatment. By the way, so you know, they both survived that night." Nora glanced toward the parking lot.

Landon felt relieved. "I'm glad to hear that. It's not my thing going around hurting people. But that doesn't explain what you said about suspecting that I had something to do with it."

Nora laughed gently. "Both of them were heavily sedated when they arrived at the hospital. One of them appeared frightened and kept talking about a wolf, a ghost-wolf he called it, that had attacked him that night. I never paid much attention to it, thinking it was only the ramblings of a medicated person, at least until the night of the Town Hall Meeting."

"I don't understand," said Landon. "What does the Town Hall Meeting have to do it?"

"Toward the end of the meeting, when Poste tried to cause some problems, you were one of the people who took a stand. And beside you, this fierce little fella had his teeth bared and was prepared to go to the end with you." She glanced down at Bob. "Weren't you, boy?" Bob wriggled in excitement at hearing his name.

Nora stepped in close to Landon, locking eyes with his, and smiled. "It didn't take a lot of serious deduction from that point."

Landon chuckled and turned toward the trail. "Well, it's a beautiful day. Shall we go for a walk?"

"Let's wait for a while. I invited Gwen Doyle to join us. You remember Gwen?"

"Of course," Landon said. "She was sure fired up at the Town Hall Meeting. She got a lot of other folks thinking as well. How has she been doing?"

"She's doing as well as can be expected, all things considered. They sent their son, Aaron, back to Newfoundland to stay with his grandmother for a while. She phoned me this morning; something about her husband, Paddy, being beaten by the militia. I thought it would be best if we had a chance to talk to her. She should be here any minute now."

"Sounds good," said Landon as he picked up a stick and threw it for Bob to fetch. Bob whipped around to go after it, then stopped, his hackles raised and a low rumble coming from his throat just as three militia members came into view around the bend in the trail.

"Easy, boy," Landon said as Nora slipped her arm through his, nudging him forward. They strolled easily along the pavement toward the militia. As they passed, Nora smiled cheerfully at them. Bob continued to glance back every so often until they disappeared from view.

After walking up the trail for a few minutes, they turned off into the bush and began to circle back.

"That was damned uncomfortable," said Landon. He glanced down and was pleased to see that Nora's arm was still interlocked with his. He noticed that she was smiling at him. He returned the smile, took a deep breath and moved forward by her side. Bob ran circles around them.

"Just a middle-aged couple and their dog out for a little walk," Nora smiled.

Gwen was waiting for them when they got back to the bridge. She appeared fidgety and was constantly peering in all directions.

"I thought they were going to see me," she said. "I was down the bank a little bit when I first saw them so I hid under the bridge. I was so afraid they were going to see me."

Nora moved in and wrapped her arms around Gwen. "Come. Let's walk and you can tell us what's going on."

They started moving down the trail slowly with Nora's arm still draped over Gwen's shoulders. Landon walked on the opposite side of her while Bob took a position in front of them.

About 20 minutes later, they arrived at the spot where Nora had first seen Landon on the trail. She turned toward the river, guiding Gwen toward the bench where she and Landon had sat and talked. As Gwen sat down, Nora noticed the memorial plaque attached to the seat back. As she turned to Landon, her features softened even more. She took a seat beside Gwen.

"It's safe here. No one is around to hear anything," Nora said.

Gwen checked behind her, then toward the trail. Her eyes began to fill. "I don't know what to do. I am so afraid. I want the people responsible for Keira's death to be punished but there's no one to turn to."

"You said something about Paddy when you phoned me earlier."

"They beat him up and left him about 30 kilometres out on the highway. He couldn't get hold of me until he had walked back to the Carcross Corner. I had to go get the car downtown to go get him. He is really badly hurt," she sobbed.

"I didn't see anything about that at the hospital," said Nora.

"He wouldn't go to the hospital. He said there's enough trouble already so he wants to keep it quiet. They told him it was because of what I said at the meeting. After he told them that he wasn't going to tell me to be quiet, that's when they beat him."

"He really should be seen by a doctor," Nora suggested. "But I understand his fears." She glanced up at Landon.

"He keeps saying he's going to get even with them," said Gwen, her tears now flowing freely. "Things have been so hard at home. He blames himself for everything but feels trapped and thinks he can't do anything about it. He's so depressed. His drinking has gotten out of hand and I'm afraid he's going to do something stupid." She leaned into Nora, resting her head on Nora's shoulder.

Landon sidled over to the other end of the bench and settled in beside Gwen.

"Do you need a safe place to go to?" he asked Gwen. "Both you and Paddy could come out to my place for a while."

Gwen raised her head. "Thank you, but I don't think that's necessary. If he would only stop getting drunk and come home to work on this with me, we could get through it together. Maybe there is nothing we can do about that mine and the poisoned water. But I'm not going to stop trying."

She turned to Nora, a renewed stream of tears dampening her face. "Is it really my fault? Am I to blame for him getting beaten up? Do I have to pretend that what happened to Keira was actually our fault simply for being where we were?"

She swung back to Landon. "What the hell happened? How did we let everything get so bad? Why is it that companies have more rights than people? What am I going to do? My little girl..." She leaned forward with her elbows on her knees, her body wracking in anguish.

Nora and Landon waited for Gwen to finish crying. Bob nuzzled between her hands and softly licked the moisture from her face. She took his face in both hands and smiled. "Thank you," she said as she wrapped her arms around his neck.

"We'll help with whatever we can," said Nora. "I'm not sure what that could be, but I can recommend someone for Paddy to talk to and I know some wonderful counsellors at the hospice who can help."

She wondered if she should tell them about the group that had been meeting at Charles's home. She decided against it as Gwen's situation was so fragile.

The four of them rose and headed back to the bridge, taking the trail along the river bank instead of the Millennium Trail. Their passage was quiet and uneventful. Landon and Nora walked with Gwen to her car.

"Call me," said Nora. "I meant it when I said I know people that can help."

Nora and Gwen hugged before Gwen drove away, heading back toward the Whitehorse city centre.

As they walked toward the parked pickup, Bob danced around Landon and Nora, wagging his tail.

"You must be getting hungry, eh, boy?" said Landon. "I'll get you something in a minute." He turned to Nora. "Man, I sure feel sorry for those two. It's really rough to lose someone."

Nora nodded. "I know."

"I'm going to give Bob something to eat. Then I guess I'll head home."

"Are you going to eat with him?"

"Naw," Landon laughed. "I'll grab something when I get home."

"My place is a lot closer," Nora smiled. "I've got some great lasagna that we could share."

Landon hesitated, thinking of everything that had taken place over the past number of days. He thought of Wenda and then believed he could feel her smiling down on him. He knew she would want him to move on with his life.

"I love lasagna," he said. As they turned to walk over to his truck he reached out and felt Nora's hand as her fingers entwined with his. "Yup, I love lasagna." He relaxed and smiled.

Galen called a meeting of the select group of friends at Charles's house a few days later. He had been staying there since the Town Hall Meeting because he thought it would be safer than remaining in his apartment at the senior's residence.

Danielle and Sherry arrived early so they could visit before the meeting began and parked their car under the roof of the woodshed as Charles suggested. They were animated as they told Charles and Galen about the intrusion from the militia. Their excitement rose to a fever pitch as they described how the neighbours and Gérard had helped them.

Galen smiled over the rim of his glasses when they gushed the news of Gérard's photos of the mine site. He listened closely as they described the evidence that those images contained.

He calmly stacked the folders that were on the table in front of him.

"This is really good news," he said. "I'm sure the others will be pleased to hear it as well." He glanced up at the old circular saw blade that had been turned into a clock. "They should be here in half an hour or so."

In the distance they heard a faint chopping sound that was progressively getting louder and louder. Charles ducked out the door and stepped out into the yard. Danielle quickly followed.

"Over there," Charles said as he pointed at the southern horizon. Danielle squinted, trying to catch sight of what he was seeing. Then she saw it, the dragonfly-like outline of a helicopter.

They ducked under the roof of the porch of the house and watched as the chopper flew a straight line toward them. As it circled the property they could make out the insignia of The Coalition on its side.

"Is that why you had us park in the woodshed?" Danielle asked. "How did you know they would be coming?"

"I didn't," Charles replied as he peered up the driveway. "I wasn't really expecting a chopper but I figured that the less visibility, the better. I wonder where Nora and Landon are. They should have been here by now. I hope everything is okay."

The helicopter banked in one direction then swivelled and circled in the opposite direction before gaining altitude and heading back south. Galen and Sherry stepped out of the garage to join Charles and Danielle on the porch.

"I don't think this is a safe place for meetings anymore," said Galen. "We're going to have to think of somewhere else."

They glanced nervously at each other as they heard the sound of a vehicle coming up the drive.

"Danielle and Sherry, you two go over behind the shed where your car is," said Galen. "Charles and I will stay here. We are who they'll be expecting."

The Frasers ran behind the woodshed and then peeked around the corner of the structure to watch the yard. They breathed a sigh of relief when they saw the rusting pickup turn the last corner into the yard. Landon had arrived, and he brought company. Danielle and Sherry ran toward the middle of the yard.

Landon threw open the door and jumped out of the truck. Bob leaped out of the back.

"Is everything okay?" he yelled at Charles.

"Everything's fine; there was a helicopter circling us but they're gone now. Where were you? We were expecting you earlier."

Nora walked around the front fender of the old Chevy. Charles and Galen watched curiously as a man unknown to them followed her.

"We drove past your yard first because there was a black four-wheel drive following us up the road," Nora said. "We went about half a kilometre further down then pulled off to a spot overlooking the river. We got out and walked around as if we were only sightseers."

"Any idea who it was?" asked Galen.

Landon walked up to him and shook his hand. "Don't know for sure, but I suspect it was militia or someone working for them." Galen peeped over Landon's shoulder at the man who was standing beside Nora. Charles had not moved.

Nora guided the man forward to meet the others. He seemed a bit hesitant.

"Gentlemen. Ladies. This is Matthieu Archibeque, Dr. Matthieu Archibeque. Dr. Archibeque has offered to be available to us should we need any medical help and don't want to go through the regular channels."

Charles frowned at her incredulously.

Nora smiled as she turned from one of her friends to the other. "It's okay. He's put himself on the line for us already. I believe he'll be a welcome member of our group." She went on to tell the story of the doctor's encounter with Stone and Kirsten.

Galen welcomed the doctor. "Anyone that Nora trusts, I'm willing to trust. Welcome, Dr. Archibeque. I hope you never regret getting to know us."

"You can call me Matt, if you don't mind...and thank you for your welcome. I hope I can be of service to your cause."

"Come, everyone, let's go into the garage," said Charles. He turned back to Landon. "Maybe you should park your truck in that little grove of trees on the side of the yard so it won't be so visible."

Landon nodded and backed the truck under the trees. He came back to the garage and was joined by Nora who stood by his side, her hand in his, touching his arm with her other hand. Galen's eyebrows arched. She smiled back at him as he grinned appreciatively.

The room went quiet at the sound of another vehicle in the yard. Sherry went to the window, peered out and then ran through the door into the yard. Danielle followed as far as the door.

"Gérard is here," said Danielle. She glanced back into the yard and laughed. "Sherry is so star-struck with this man. He's the photographer we were telling you about, Galen."

After backing his vehicle into the woods beside Landon's truck, at Sherry's suggestion, Gérard joined the rest inside. Nora made a pot of coffee and Sherry introduced Gérard to the rest of the group. The feeling of camaraderie built as they sat around the table chatting. Galen broke the reverie and suggested that they get on with the discussion that they had gotten together for.

"Perhaps we can learn more about the photos that Sherry has told us about?" he said, directing his question at Gérard.

Gérard smiled and spent the next fifteen minutes showing the photographs of the mine to the group and explaining what they would prove.

After he finished, Galen perused the room, catching the eye of each individual as he went past them, waiting to see if there were any questions.

"This could be what we need to turn this whole mess from a mining and oil and gas exploration affair into a criminal matter," he said. "If we can do that, we get to bypass the militia and deal with the RCMP."

Galen then held up a copy of a magazine. All eyes turned toward him.

"Do any of you subscribe to the *Current Chronicle*? It's a very enlightened, informative news magazine published by a non-profit organization. They often have some very controversial articles."

Charles glanced at his old friend. "I take it there's a reason you're asking us, Galen? Surely you haven't deviated off the topic." He smiled.

"No," laughed Galen. "My mind hasn't wandered. This latest issue has a remarkable story written by a young journalist who happens to live right here in Whitehorse. It has a wonderful title. She's called it *Fracking Ridiculous*. It's an in-depth study of the damage caused by hydraulic fracturing throughout Yukon, and hints at similar issues throughout the rest of Canada, and indeed all of North America."

"That will get her some attention, some of it unwanted," said Charles. "Who is this writer?"

"Her name is Kirsten Allerton," said Galen. "She's a very persuasive correspondent; always able to verify her content." He paused, a mischievous grin on his face.

"There is one more thing," he said. "In her essay she brought up the fact that there is a mining operation operating so close to Whitehorse that it may present a hazard to the population. Gérard's photos are further attestation of everything she wrote about."

Nora's eyes met Landon's. "Landon and I know her," Nora said. "We had no idea she was writing an article on the situation here. She and her partner, Stone, are quite a remarkable young couple. We may hear more from them as time goes on."

They took turns skimming through the article and chatting about its content. When they returned to their chairs and were seated around the table again, Landon opened the conversation.

His eyebrows dropped into a small frown as he began. "I got a call from Wolfgang Grimm's executive assistant. I think she said her name was Mahalia. I have no way of knowing whether the call was genuine or not but she passed on a warning that she had overheard Chong, Poste and others saying they were going to put an end to any kind of meetings such as the Town Hall Meeting. In particular, they intend to come after any of us that were involved in that one."

"How can we trust her?" asked Charles. "After all, she works for the people we are fighting against. And why did she call you? Wouldn't they be more interested in Galen and me?"

Landon turned to Nora and then back to Charles. "Apparently, she heard the story of the 'phantom wolf' as well and when she saw Bob and me at the meeting she assumed that I was more involved than it first appeared. I'm not sure how she got my name, but she seems to be very resourceful." He explained to the others how Nora had connected him and Bob with the mine incident.

"I'm trusting my gut feeling on this one," he continued. "I think we need to pay attention to her warning." He stood, walked over to the window and leaned on the sill, gazing through the glass. "I hope we can stop them before something else goes wrong," he said to no one in particular. He turned to the others in the room. Nora got up and moved to stand beside him, her arm around his waist.

"So, what's the next step, folks?" he asked.

Chapter 15

A plume of black smoke belched from the Peterbilt's exhaust stacks as Josh brought the powerful diesel through the curves and began climbing the 8% rise in the highway known as Jackson's Hill. There was a lookout at the top where he would be able to turn off and take a break after seven straight hours of driving from the mine. He felt a surge of joy as he pushed down the throttle to keep the containers with 21,000 kilograms of ore moving upward. He loved being in control of that much power.

Who would've believed that little Joshua Parsons from Trinity, Newfoundland could be making this much money and giving so much to Beth and the kids, he thought. He crested the top of the climb and pulled into the viewpoint. He slid out of his seat, down the step and then walked over to the guard rail, overlooking a section of the Tintina Trench a bit south of Stewart Crossing.

In the distance he could barely make out the flags that were flying on the top of the oil and gas rigs that dotted the low-lying plain. He was thinking of those damned environmentalists who had tried to stop development in this area. *They're stunned as me arse*, he thought. *There's a lot of people working because of all of this. All kinds of money has been taken outta here. Oil and gas exploration is good for the economy. Mmm-hmm, this is the best thing that's ever happened to me.*

He walked back to the big rig and climbed back into the cockpit. He was anxious to get to the next stretch of road as it was a gradual decline into the lower reaches of the Trench and he would be able to make some good time. He was looking forward to getting home to Carmacks.

The massive starter shook the huge PACCAR MX engine as it cranked up to starting speed. Another belch of black smoke and the 18-wheeler was ready to roll again. He dropped it into gear, released the air brakes and cranked the shiny red behemoth back onto the road. He started humming the tune to "Missing Home Today" and a moment later broke into full song.

The truck lurched precipitously toward the side of the road. He held tight to the steering wheel as he brought it back toward centre.

The sound of tires screaming and air from the brakes hissing echoed through the valley below as Josh wrestled the truck to a stop. He squinted, then his brow furrowed as complete disbelief ran through him. The road ahead was undulating—moving up and down like a gymnast's ribbon. Unbelievably, the motion was headed toward him.

He was glued to his seat, terrified and locked in by the seatbelt when it hit. The groan of twisting metal and the crash of breaking glass went unheard as the roar of the trees and rocks being thrown about drowned out all other sound. He stared, unblinking, as the truck was raised 10 metres, then dumped on its side to roll into an ever-expanding maw of moving earth.

It was over less than a minute later. The truck was right side up, crushed in from all directions and separated from the B-Train load it had been pulling. Josh rolled his eyes to look around, barely able to breathe. The truck was facing up the hill and he could see about 25 metres up the bank to where the road had once been. All that remained was an overhang of chip seal.

Tears filled his eyes as he thought of his family. Sarah and Eddie would be helping Beth get ready for little

Pete's second birthday. The celebration was to begin when Josh got home. He reached down and undid the clasp of the seatbelt and tried to open the door. It was too damaged to swing open.

He noticed that the windshield had been broken out of the truck and saw that as an avenue of escape. As he went to pull himself up he realized that his legs were trapped by the dashboard and metal that had been pushed to the seat. He was curious why he didn't feel that.

It's only a matter of time, he thought. *They know I was on the road so they'll be coming to get me soon.* He leaned back in the seat and closed his eyes in prayer. The truck moved. It began to shake and vibrate with the aftershock. Josh's eyes opened as he felt something touch his hand. He glanced down to see that the picture of Beth and the kids had been jostled from above the visor and had fallen into his lap. He smiled.

Then another, heavier, shaking hit the truck. His eyes grew wide as he stared through the open windshield and watched as ground gave way, releasing thousands of tons of roadway and dirt down the bank toward him. His scream of terror was silenced by the debris that filled the cab of the truck.

Meanwhile in Carmacks, Beth, seven-year-old Sarah, and four-year-old Eddie were busily preparing for Pete's birthday celebration when the house began to shake. Sarah held onto Pete while Eddie rushed to his mother's side. They hurried to stand under the archway to the living room to wait for the tremor to stop.

"Mommy, I'm scared," said Eddie as he hung onto her leg.

"It'll be okay, honey, it's only a little earthquake," she replied as she drew her other two children near. "It'll stop in a few seconds."

The disturbing movement of the house slowed, and then stopped completely. Beth quickly checked to see if there was any apparent damage to the house. Seeing none, she encouraged the children to come back to the kitchen to continue making the goodies for the birthday party.

A short time later, the floor began to feel like it was buckling again. They returned to the perceived safety of the archway and watched as items on the tables and shelves in the living room were jostled and moved around. As the movement stopped, a photograph fell from the mantel and crashed onto the stone hearth. Beth got a broom and dust pan and went to clean up the broken glass. When she turned the frame over, the torn picture of a very proud Josh standing beside his truck came into view.

The huge teak desk no longer felt like a sanctuary for Wolfgang Grimm since Sam Chong had taken over completely following his arrival in Whitehorse. He sat in his chair nursing yet another scotch as he recalled the events of the last meeting with Chong, Melody Lloyd and Josef Poste. He found it disturbing that their focus was on covering their tracks and seeking revenge on the people who had organized the Town Hall Meeting instead of on making sure there were no more similar incidences. He was losing patience with Chong's arrogant attitude and disturbing behaviour.

He pressed the button on the intercom and asked Mahalia to come into his office. He averted his eyes as she slipped into the room, in an attempt to keep his mind on business instead of her beautiful appearance.

"Mahalia, I need to get hold of The Capitol. I'm concerned about what actions Chong and Poste may be planning."

Something felt like a bump underneath his chair, and then the nauseating motion of the building moving caused him to place both hands flat on his desk as if to hold everything steady. Mahalia slipped and stumbled to the floor, her skirt rising up her thigh. Again, he averted his eyes.

His attention was drawn to the rattling and clinking at the bar. He watched as several glasses and bottles tumbled to the floor. His pushed his chair back as he jumped up and ran around the desk to Mahalia. The shaking stopped as he reached her.

"Are you okay, Mahalia?"

"Yes. I slipped off of my heels. Everything's okay."

He helped her get back on her feet as their eyes connected.

"As long as you're sure," he said. "I wouldn't want anything to happen to you."

She smiled and gave him a buss on the cheek. "Thank you, Wolfgang. But I assure you everything is fine. Wow. That was the biggest earthquake I've felt since I left the Bahamas."

"I never felt anything like that here before," said Grimm. "I wonder where the epicentre was," he added as an afterthought.

"We'll hear soon enough," she said. "I better make sure all the communication systems are up and running. We're bound to get some instructions from Vancouver as soon as they hear about this."

171

She turned and moved out the door to go back to her desk. Grimm watched as her snug skirt and sleeveless blouse left the room...this time he didn't turn away.

The glasses started to tinkle again. He heard a crash to his left and scowled when he saw that a painting had plunged to the floor.

The tent was not as comfortable as Charles's garage, but it served the purpose and allowed meetings to take place unobtrusively. The trip to Landon's property was more onerous for Galen because of the rough terrain but he had suggested it as a matter of safety after he learned that Landon had a large camouflage canvas tent in storage.

Landon was in the yard, casually throwing the ball for Bob to fetch. Galen and Charles had arrived with Nora fifteen minutes earlier and they were waiting for the others to arrive. Nora went into the cabin and made a pot of coffee.

It was another half-hour before they saw the grill of Gérard's Jeep as it came out of the trail into the open space. The doors of the car opened and people spilt out in all directions. Danielle, Sherry, Kirsten and Stone had all come with him.

They went into the tent and started taking seats around the table. Nora came in with the pot of coffee and a number of cups on a tray. Unexpectedly, Bob brushed past her and ran to where Landon was seated. She was knocked off balance and dropped the tray onto the ground.

"Bob!" said Landon. "What is wrong with you?" He rushed to Nora. "Are you okay? Did you get hurt?"

The others were standing in front of their chairs straining to see Nora picking up the coffee pot and cups.

"I'm fine. Sorry about the coffee. I wonder what got into Bob?"

Before Landon could respond, the canvas walls began flapping back and forth. The earth beneath their feet shuddered and felt like it was being pulled from underneath them. They braced themselves against the stomach-turning movement. Galen fell to his hands and knees.

When it was over, Charles helped Galen to his feet.

"I wonder where that one came from?" said Landon.

"Have you ever felt one that strong before?" asked Gérard. "In all my time here I have not."

"No, I don't think I ever have. Galen, what about you?"

Galen regained his composure and then sat in a chair resting his arms on the table.

"This might be what I have been afraid of. I have spoken at length about the dangers involved with fracking and disturbing the inner layers of the earth. God, I hope this doesn't mean my fears have come to fruition."

They sat chatting about their experiences with earthquakes for a time before Landon reminded them that they were meeting in order to decide how to move forward in dealing with the issues of water safety and The Coalition.

As they began that conversation, Bob ran to Landon's side again and whined, his ears laid back.

Landon grinned at the others at the table. "Something tells me we're about to feel an aftershock," he said as he patted Bob's side.

Their world began moving again.

The inhabitants of the communities in the low-lying areas of the Tintina Trench experienced a nightmare of events that none of them could have imagined previously. Buildings collapsed, bridges had fallen, airstrips had broken up and there were multiple injuries.

The shock of the earthquake travelled through the entire Tintina Trench and carried on through the Rocky Mountain Trench. People reported feeling it as far away as Edmonton.

This would be hard to keep quiet.

Chapter 16

The government-operated press on both radio and television reported a medium strength earthquake that was centred toward the middle of Yukon, and included assurances that there was little to no damage incurred anywhere. The official line was that it was a natural, common occurrence that had been expected for a long time. There was no need to worry.

Information filtering through the Internet, telephone calls and ham radio operators gave a somewhat different, bleak, outlook. They talked about it being a massive 9.3 earthquake that they claimed took place just south of Stewart Crossing and that roadways were destroyed, oil and gas rigs toppled and that underground mines had collapsed.

Within two days, a desperate call was made by Mayo, Stewart Crossing, Faro and Ross River asking that Central Yukon be declared a disaster area and for the government to evacuate everyone. The entire region resembled a war zone and was going to be flooded by the altered course of the rivers. They wanted help before it was too late.

The official government position, as dictated by The Coalition, was that it was nothing to worry about. The residents of those communities and of the outlying areas started trying to find their own way out. There were no roads that had been left undamaged. Some tried to leave by riverboat but quickly found that some of the larger rivers, the Liard River and the Pelly River were completely choked off. There was no way out by water.

Another day passed before the general population of Whitehorse and southern Canada became fully aware of the grave situation those communities faced. People muttered to each other about the irresponsibility of government and The Coalition and as they did so, their anger grew.

At noon on the fifth day, a number of men began to congregate on Main Street. What began as a small gathering of friends and acquaintances rapidly became a constantly expanding group of angry people. Within two hours, the mob numbered around 100 and the agitators within were creating a mentality that was absent of reasonable thought.

A woman they recognized from the Town Hall Meeting moved up the steps of the federal building at the corner of Third and Main, where she could be seen and heard by everyone. As she took her place above the crowd, the yelling and murmuring became muted, and then stopped as she raised both hands in the air and they all looked toward her in anticipation.

"We've been letting them do what they want for decades," said Gwen. "It's time we take back our community—and our lives. Some of us have experienced unimaginable losses. Most of you know that we lost our daughter to them. But all of us have lost our freedom and our rights as Canadians."

"They're lying to us, the bastards," shouted a young, heavily tattooed man. "They've been lying to us all along!"

"We should kill the sons of bitches!" shouted another.

Once more Gwen interrupted the disturbance with an upraised hand. Again, the crowd quieted to hear what she had to say.

"Nobody wants to get even more than I do. Nobody wants to make them hurt more than I do. But if we don't take the right approach to this they'll just bring in more militia and force us to stop."

"Then, what are we supposed to do?" asked a woman in the front of the group. "We can't do nothing."

Landon jostled his way through the amassed mob until he reached the steps on which Gwen stood. He moved up to stand beside her. Bob was waiting for him in the truck.

"I think what Gwen is trying to tell you is that we have to keep priorities in sequence. Do not let your frustration and anger take away from the immediate need. What we need to do right now is get help to those communities that have been hit so heavily by this disaster. We need to convince President Grimm that The Coalition must provide assistance in getting everyone to safety."

A burly man in a mackinaw pushed his way through the crowd. "How the hell do you expect to do that?" he growled. "That son of a bitch hasn't done anything for us since he got here."

Gwen gazed down at the man. "That may be true, but we have to think beyond our own anger in order to act in a way that will help those poor people. Without help they cannot survive. There is no clean water. There's not even any animals left to hunt in that area."

"Yeah, the fucking oil and gas and mining companies made damn sure of that, didn't they?" came a voice from the back. "I say we go over there and pull that son of a bitch out of his office. Then we'll see how quick he is to do what we tell him."

A number of people in the mob turned to look across the street at the top floor of the building on Fourth and Main where Grimm's office was located. Some started to move in that direction.

"Stop!" shouted Landon. "That place is a fortress and you're not going to get in. There are armed militia on every level and the top floor was designed to be impenetrable from below. Don't waste valuable time by letting your anger get the best of you."

The tattooed man that had spoken earlier moved toward the front.

"What do you propose we do? Go in and ask nicely? Do any of us believe that would work?" He moved two steps up, and then turned to the crowd. "I say we go drag the bastard out now."

He moved off the steps and started pushing his way angrily through the crowd of onlookers. "Come on! Follow me!" he bellowed, his eyes focused on the doorway to the building ahead.

He kept looking backward over his shoulder as he stormed across the street. Just as he got to the sidewalk on the other side he turned incredulously to the gathering.

"What the hell is wrong with you? Come on! Let's get him!"

He turned toward the building again and was brought to an abrupt halt by the barrel of an assault rifle that was jammed into his chest with enough force to knock him head over heels. Behind the militia man who had just felled him, he could see that the entire sidewalk was filled with armed guards fully outfitted in riot gear. He scrambled backward, turning to rise to his feet and run back to the safety of the crowd.

Landon touched Gwen's arm and connected with her eyes. She nodded and then turned to move down the steps with him. The crowd parted, creating a pathway toward the army on the other side.

The large, trench coat-clad man with the classic AK-47 stepped forward to meet them.

"Nobody comes across the street," he said when they got within hearing distance.

Landon and Gwen continued moving toward him, walking slowly and looking directly into his eyes. They stopped a meter in front of him.

"Please tell President Grimm that Landon McGuire and Gwendolyn Doyle request an audience with him," said Landon quietly.

"Nobody comes across the street," he replied. "That's my orders."

"We're not asking you to go against your orders, Sir," said Gwen. "We are simply asking that you let President Grimm know that we would like to speak with him."

The man considered them for a moment, and then signalled one of his cohorts to come forward.

"Tell the President that these two want to see him," he ordered. He turned back to Landon and Gwen. "If he says no, that's the end of it."

The man who had gone to see Grimm returned about 5 minutes later. He nodded to his commander. "President Grimm says he'll see you," the man said. "Follow me."

Landon turned back to search the exponentially expanding crowd to find Charles, Galen, and Gérard. He felt assured by their nods toward him that they would try and keep the crowd under control. He knew that Nora, Danielle and Sherry were in the middle of the crowd to assist and Stone was off to one side as well as Kirsten who was busily putting pencil to paper in her notepad. He turned back to Gwen and they strode across the street and through the armoured doors.

Once the elevator door closed, Gwen turned to Landon. "Thank you for stepping in. I don't know what would've happened if you didn't."

"It just seems to me that together we could be more convincing than either one of us alone," he smiled back at her. "Now, if we can just do the same with Grimm."

They stepped into the small alcove between the elevator and the office and as the doors swung inward, Mahalia greeted them into the outer office.

"President Grimm will be with you in a moment," she said, averting eye contact with Landon. "Please, have a seat. Can I get you anything? Perhaps a coffee or a glass of water?"

Both Gwen and Landon declined the offer as they took seats on the richly upholstered sofa. Mahalia turned and moved through the ornate door to the inner office.

"I can only imagine what the inside of that office looks like," said Gwen. "Look at those doors."

Landon sat back and crossed his legs, his eyes taking in every detail of the room.

The door to the inner sanctum opened again and Mahalia invited them inside. As they stepped through the door they were both dumbstruck by the opulence of the room that Grimm called his office. Everything about it spelt extravagance. Mahalia guided them to the two chairs that sat facing Grimm's expansive desk.

Grimm peered down at them from behind his desk. "How can I help you, Mr. Maguire, Mrs. Doyle?"

"I think you know why we are here," Landon said. "Otherwise you never would have agreed to see us. President Grimm, there needs to be a solution to the

From Thine Own Well

situation in the communities that have been heavily affected by the earthquake. We believe the only chance they have is for The Coalition to provide the necessary equipment and manpower to evacuate them from the area."

"Don't you think that's up to your government?"

Gwen's eyes burned as her head snapped up to look at him. "The Coalition hasn't left enough of the government to do anything to help," she said. "The leaders are only puppets and there isn't enough public servants left to do much of anything. Those people need your help."

Gwen glared over the teak desk and refused to break eye contact with him. Grimm finally looked away.

"Listen," he said. "I understand what you're saying and I sympathize with those folks who are having difficulties, but there's really not much that I can do."

Landon stood and leaned forward until his face was only centimetres away from Grimm's.

"You can get hold of The Capitol and demand that they send help."

Grimm moved back to his chair, uneasy. "What makes you think they would listen to me? I really don't see the point in even trying to get them involved. They've already said it's the government's responsibility."

"You are aware that there will be criminal charges laid from all this, right?" Landon said as he returned to his seat.

Grimm's eyebrows rose. "What do you mean criminal charges? An earthquake is a natural phenomenon; nobody is liable for an earthquake."

"Unless they were involved in behaviour that caused the earthquake," said Gwen. "Or allowed behaviour that caused the earthquake...like fracking."

Grimm guffawed nervously. "Fracking goes on all over the world. Nobody's ever been blamed for an earthquake."

Landon glanced toward Gwen, and then stood up again. He leaned on Grimm's desk and stared directly into the President's eyes.

"Listen. There are over 2000 people in danger. The only way they can get help is for The Coalition to do what has to be done. What do you think is going to happen when the rest of the country learns that you, President Grimm, stood by and did nothing while all those people perished?"

"And there's more," said Gwen. "It may well be that The Coalition will be seen to be involved in other criminal activity as well."

"What the hell are you talking about?" burst out Grimm. "The Coalition sets the rules and says what's okay with oil and gas exploration and what isn't. Nobody's going to be able—"

"No one can poison water and get away with it," snapped Gwen. "There's much more involved than just this earthquake and you know it. You had better get on the phone and start getting some help or there will be hell to pay."

Grimm jumped at the tone of her voice. He was not used to having people talk to him in that manner. He was about to tell her so when Landon slapped his palm on top of the desk.

"Trust me," Landon said. "We have enough evidence on the GroundSave Mining operation for criminal charges to be laid on several people, perhaps even including you. When geologists are able to show that the oil and gas fracking in the Tintina Trench was what caused this earthquake, and evidence shows that The Coalition tried to minimize everything, a lot more criminal charges are going to be laid."

Perspiration started to form on Grimm's forehead. His right eye began to twitch.

"Even if The Coalition is charged with something under the Criminal Code, the most that could come out of it would be some fines," Grimm said. "They're not going to spend hundreds of thousands more when they think they can blame the government."

Landon leaned in even closer. "You're not getting it, Grimm," he growled. "They will make sure that there's somebody to take the fall for them. Who do you think that will be? Who has been given the responsibility of The Coalition's activities in Yukon?" He stepped back from the desk and looked around the office.

"When all is said and done you will be hung out to dry, and all of this," he made a broad gesture around the room with his hand, "will mean nothing. You are going to end up as the scapegoat."

Grimm regarded the two of them, and his eyes filled with fear. He had seen it before so he knew that The Coalition would do whatever it had to do to protect itself. He knew that he could very easily become the patsy.

"I'm not sure what I can do," he said softly. "I don't know how I could get them to mobilize everything necessary to conduct an evacuation of this magnitude. There is a huge area to cover."

"Present it as a matter of international public relations," said Landon. "They will be able to show the world how they are truly a great corporate citizen and at the same time maybe they can lessen the animosity that they have created in Canada."

Gwen softened her approach toward Grimm. "You have an opportunity to do something wonderful right here, right now," she said. "Think of all those people, the elders, the small children...and then do what is right."

Grimm sighed. "I'll have to give it some thought," he said. "I need some time."

"Time is running out," said Landon. "I suggest you do something quickly or you're also going to have to deal with the results of people's anger right here in Whitehorse as well."

Grimm's shoulders slouched in resignation. He reached for the button on the intercom.

"Mahalia, please connect me with the President of the Department of Peace and Well Being in Vancouver. Oh, and arrange for my jet to be prepared for a flight down there."

He looked up at Landon and Gwen. "Now if you'll excuse me?" he said as he rose and gestured toward the door.

Gwen and Landon pushed through the doors into the outer office, startling Mahalia who was already on the phone. They went straight to the elevator and then out onto the street. They made their way across the street through the crowd and climbed to the top of the steps where they had been before.

This time it was Landon who raised his hands to address the crowd. "President Grimm is contacting The Capitol as we speak. We'll know within hours whether they will actually do something or not," he said to them. "All we can do now is wait and see what the result is."

"Well, they better fucking do something," called a voice from the crowd.

They started to disperse in small groups. There was still much discussion and murmuring going on as they gawked back toward Grimm's office. Nora ran up the steps and hugged Landon. She then turned and wrapped her arms around Gwen.

Charles, Galen, Danielle and Sherry, Stone and Kirsten, and Gérard joined them at the top of the steps.

"I have some news," said Kirsten. "I got a phone call from the RCMP just before I came down here. They were asking about my *Current Chronicle* article. They wanted to know if I had information I could share that wouldn't put my source in danger."

"And, what did you tell them?" asked Galen.

Kirsten smiled as Stone put his arm around her. "I expect to see them early next week," she said.

Chapter 17

For the first time since she was hired by Grimm, Mahalia was feeling uncomfortable as she walked into the office and sat at her desk. Chong had called about an hour after Wolfgang had spoken to the President of the Department of Peace and Well Being in Vancouver. He had demanded that Grimm wait at the office until he and the others got there. She glanced over her shoulder at the nameplate on the door to the inner office. *I wonder what they're going to try and push Wolfgang into,* she wondered. *Chong was so angry when he called. What did he expect? Wolfgang had to take steps to save all those people.*

She got up from her desk and went into Grimm's office. He was sitting at his desk with his head in his hands, not moving.

"Wolfgang?"

He lifted his head to look at her. He had the look of a man who was totally exhausted and appeared to be using every effort he had just to stay alert.

"Are you okay?" she asked. "Silly question, I know," she said as she moved behind him and began massaging his shoulders and neck. "They're going to be here any minute. You might want to freshen up and get ready for them."

He said nothing as he stood out in his chair and walked over to the walk-in closet by the washroom. He turned back to her.

"Thank you. Thank you for all your help."

Then he stepped inside and pulled the door closed behind him. Mahalia busied herself making coffee and arranging cups on the serving tray. She had just finished setting the chairs around a conference table when she heard the door of the outer office open. A chill went up her spine.

Chong did not wait for her to come out to escort him into the office. He stormed straight in, followed by Melody Lloyd, Tom Alexander and Josef Poste. They hesitated, almost bumping into each other when Chong stopped abruptly and looked around the office.

"He'll be right with you," Mahalia said as she forced a smile. "Have a seat in the conference room. The coffee is ready and you can let me know if you need anything else."

Chong turned and walked quickly into the conference room and then started walking back and forth at the head of the table. The others went directly to the chairs and sat down, all eyes fixed on the outer office looking for Grimm.

He was wearing a freshly dry-cleaned suit, shirt and silk tie when he arrived. The look was topped off with patent leather shoes and a single white rose as a boutonniere. He walked past Chong at the head of the table and pulled the chair out. He studied Chong's eyes, then sat in the chair and turned it to face the table.

"Have a seat, Sam," he said, indicating the chair further down the table. "What can I do for you?"

Chong was perplexed. He was not used to being treated in that fashion. He continued to pace at the head of the table behind Grimm's chair until he realized the absurdity of his action. He moved down the room but pushed a chair out of the way and remained standing as he turned back to the head of the table.

"What the hell are you doing calling Vancouver without talking to me first?" he snarled at Grimm. "What makes you think I'm going to stand for that kind of insolence?"

Grimm remained unruffled. He looked around at the others in the room with a wry grin, and then focused directly on Chong.

"Are you telling me that you wanted to be the one to ask The Capitol for help? You wanted to be the one to explain how there was over a couple thousand people in danger that you wanted to see saved? If that's the case, I apologize."

Grimm's casual, relaxed appearance disappeared as he stood quickly and leaned forward, putting both hands on the table top. "But if you are telling me that you were not going to allow that call to be made, then you can go fuck yourself."

His eyes darted over to see Mahalia standing in the doorway and then he turned his attention back to Chong. Mahalia had never seen Grimm acting in this fashion. His relaxed, calm demeanour had dropped like loosened armour from a knight's back.

"Do you think that I got here by letting people like you push me around?" he roared. "Trust me, when it comes to protecting the reputation of The Coalition, I will stop at nothing. And part of that is going to be making sure everyone is evacuated safely. Do you understand that?"

"How dare you talk to me like that," Chong retorted.

Grimm snapped his attention away from Chong and directed it at Lloyd. His icy stare caused her to squirm in her seat. She passed looks between Chong and Alexander before returning her concentration to Grimm.

"And what have you got to say?" Grimm said as he continued looking at her, unblinking.

"I'm not sure what you mean," she said. "I, I mean, GroundSave Mining has nothing to do with this earthquake. There's no way we could have caused that problem."

"That's true. But, as it turns out, there is, apparently, enough evidence to convict you and your company on criminal matters to do with poisoning the water in the Whitehorse area."

He walked over behind the chairs where Lloyd and Alexander sat. One by one he turned them around to face him.

"That sets a very bad precedent," he said as he glared down at the two of them. "A precedent that The Coalition never wanted to see happen. They are very unhappy with you."

Lloyd tried to turn her chair back toward the table; Grimm stopped the motion by placing his hand on its back. She slumped down in the chair, her wide eyes turned up at him.

"We've done everything we possibly can," she said. "We've closed down the operation and flushed out everywhere where water flowed including the creek bed. It wasn't my fault, it was a mistake."

Grimm leaned over and put his hands on both armrests of her chair; his face mere centimetres from hers as he stared directly into her eyes.

"Do you remember a little company called Windfall Mining? Do you remember that company having to clear out of Canada altogether because they poisoned water that flowed by a small community? There were a couple of deaths there too, if my information is accurate."

She shrunk even further down as he stood erect and frowned down at her again. Then he turned and walked to the head of the table again.

"For those of you who don't know, our Ms. Melody Lloyd was the corporate president of Windfall Mining during that fiasco as well. It seems she makes a habit of poisoning people's water."

He waited a moment for that information to sink in before he continued.

"The way I see it, you cannot make the same mistake twice. The second time you do something it's no longer a mistake; it's a conscious choice you are making. And you two," he said, pointing at Lloyd and Alexander, "made the choice to put people's lives in danger by poisoning water…and now a child is dead."

"But, water is being polluted all over the Yukon," stammered Lloyd.

"Perhaps," snarled Grimm. "But always be careful to make sure we are nowhere near a community so that direct contamination of their water source is not traced back to a resource company. You broke that cardinal rule."

Alexander's eyes flicked back and forth between Lloyd and Grimm.

"But The Coalition will make sure that we're protected because of *The Agreement*. Isn't that correct?" he said.

Grimm turned his eyes slowly toward Alexander; his lip began to curl upward.

"You and your company are on your own if anything more comes from your actions. The Coalition stays away from anyone who gets themselves involved in criminal matters."

Chong stepped forward and broke into the conversation.

"Poste and his men could arrest everyone that was involved. I know that fucking guy and his dog have something to do with it. I knew it as soon as I saw them at that damn Town Hall Meeting. We'll make sure that they don't bother us again."

Poste sat in his chair wide-eyed at Chong's suggestion. His eyes narrowed and his lips curved into a sneer as Chong returned to his chair.

"Just say the word and we'll look after it," he spouted.

Grimm slammed his fist on the table. "You will do nothing, you little piece of slime!" he barked. "You will leave everyone alone until this disaster has been dealt with the way The Coalition says it will be dealt with."

Chong jumped up from his chair, furious. His action startled everyone in the room except Grimm. "I will do whatever I think is necessary to do. No one, not you or anyone else will tell me any different!" His voice was shrill and uncontrolled. He headed toward the door. "Poste! Get your ass out of that chair and let's go!"

Poste stood, his eyes flashing back and forth between Grimm and Chong, visibly shaken and unsure of himself.

"You have a choice to make," Grimm said quietly.

"Poste!" Chong snapped. "I said move it; let's go."

Poste turned his eyes to the floor and with his head down followed Chong toward the doorway where Mahalia stood. She stepped back as they stormed through the outer office through the doors and into the elevator. She turned back to look at the three remaining occupants of the room. She smiled to herself as she heard Grimm talk to Lloyd and Alexander.

"You better hope that nothing more comes from your stupidity," Grimm smirked. "But, like I said, if it does you're on your own. You might want to put all your affairs in order."

He watched with disgust as Lloyd and Alexander gathered themselves and left the office. He grinned at Mahalia.

"Thank you, Mahalia," he said. "It did me a world of good to know that you are supporting me. I'm not sure what I would do without you."

"You're welcome," Mahalia smiled. Then she turned to leave the doorway and returned to her desk.

Grimm's eyes traced her shape up and down as she walked away. She turned out of sight and then he walked to the outer office.

"Would you like to get some dinner?" he asked after a moment's hesitation.

Mahalia's eyebrows furrowed slightly and her lips pursed as she considered the invitation. Then her eyes turned demurely up to him.

"I would love to."

"I don't get it," said Sherry to the others at the table. She was sitting with Danielle, Nora, Galen, Charles and Landon in the coffee shop at the end of Main Street near the river. "How can they be allowed to pollute water like that? I mean really, the government wouldn't allow that, would they?"

Galen smiled at her naivety. The others at the table waited, knowing he was going to respond. They all leaned forward so as not to miss a word.

"Actually, it was the Canadian government's myopic view of the world that created the situation where there were no longer protections in place for most major waters and waterways in Canada. Sounds crazy, doesn't it?

It was during my amendments to the *Navigable Waters Protection Act* way back in 2012. Prior to that amendment, approximately 32,000 lakes were protected from being polluted and having the sludge from mining operations adulterate the water. When the amendment came into force, only 97 lakes were left safeguarded." He locked eyes with each of his companions, one at a time. "Not one lake in Yukon made that list. Only the Yukon River was included."

Landon leaned back and crossed his legs; he rested his hands on his lap and quietly shook his head. "What that means, Sherry," he said quietly, "is that it opened everything up so there is no restriction on development simply to safeguard water. The resource companies can build bridges, dam waters, or do almost anything they want to. There's nothing left to stop them. Even the pipelines did not have to have environmental assessments considered."

"You mean it was The Coalition that did that?"

Galen slowly shook his head as he answered. "No, it was one of Canada's last officially elected governments that made that choice—the same one that signed *The Agreement*."

"Well, that's just stupid," Sherry exclaimed as she picked up her latte and sipped gingerly at the lip of the cup. "Just really stupid."

Nora smiled, understanding the young woman's disgust. She toyed with her peppermint tea for a moment and then asked if anyone had heard from Kirsten and Stone. No one had seen them since the gathering in front of Grimm's office.

Landon raised his head when he heard Bob bark from inside the pickup that was parked on Main Street in front of the coffee shop. He glanced out the window and saw two men from the militia, one on each side of the cab, looking in. He hurried out of his seat and ran outdoors, with Charles close behind him.

"Is there a problem, gentlemen?" he asked as he strode toward them, his hands touching the handle of the 44 Magnum on his hip. The man closest to him stepped back from the truck and the other came around and stood in front of the bumper. "I asked you if there was a problem," Landon repeated, the edge to his voice getting sharper.

People began spilling out of the coffee shop onto the sidewalk. The commotion had also attracted the attention of onlookers from across the street. Charles walked past them and stepped in behind the car that was parked beside Landon's pickup. He stood quietly at the back bumper and watched the scene unfold further, his right hand in his pocket.

"No problem," said the man near the driver's door as he rubbernecked nervously about. "We were just admiring your dog."

The man at the front of the truck slowly slid his trench coat back until his handgun came into view. Landon kept his body facing the first man and turned his eyes to the one reaching into his coat.

"I don't think you want to do that in front of a bunch of witnesses," Landon said to him. "Besides, you don't know how many of them might be armed," he added, nodding toward the gathering throng.

By that time, a very agitated crowd had gathered around Landon. The uniformed man that was by the door moved toward the front of the truck and then crossed in front of it and nudged his companion to move along with him. They walked toward the river, then turned the corner and were out of sight.

A cheer went up from the people who were there to watch the confrontation. They parted as they slapped Landon on the back, congratulating him as he walked back into the coffee shop, Charles quietly following. Landon sat back at the table and returned to holding his coffee cup in both hands, slowly turning it around and around.

Galen tapped his fingers on the table to get his friends' attention and then quickly looked around the table.

"I think we should call everyone together again," he said. "I'd like to make sure everyone is okay and then put our heads together about what our next move should be. The behaviour of the militia toward those we have been working with is beginning to concern me."

"Maybe we could just get everyone to come here, to the coffee shop," said Danielle. "That would be quicker and easier to do than going all the way up to Landon's."

"I'll call the rest and see if we can get everybody here sometime next week," said Charles, who had been sitting uncharacteristically quiet throughout the meeting. Landon glanced over at him and was about to nod his approval when he noticed the bulge in Charles's right pocket. He quickly brought his eyes up to meet Charles's. He leaned over and whispered.

"You came here armed?"

Charles smiled sheepishly and shrugged his shoulders. "You just never know who you will meet," he grinned.

Chapter 18

Nora, Landon and Galen arrived at the Fleming residence in Nora's Subaru station wagon. Charles had called to say that he would have some information for them that might prove to be very useful. His reticence about discussing it over the phone was caused by the certainty that all phones, both landline and wireless, were being tapped by the authorities. It appeared quiet in the yard as they came to a stop. In the back of the car Bob lifted his head, scenting the air. He began to growl.

Landon grabbed his Winchester from the seat beside him and slipped out of the back door, leaving it open as Bob followed him. He moved quickly to the open door of the garage and stood with his back against the wall. He took the rifle in both hands, then spun around and charged through the door running low, his eyes taking in everything as he moved.

"Whoa, man," Charles exclaimed from the counter where the coffee pot stood. "What's got you all riled up?"

Landon stopped and stood up, letting his grip on the firearm relax. He took a quick look around the room and smiled.

"Bob seemed to think there was something wrong here…and when I saw the garage door open I guess I just thought the worst. He probably smelled something in the bush. I'm glad everything is okay though."

He walked over to the door and signalled to the other two that it was safe to come in. He turned around to see Bob with his front paws on Charles's lap, getting his ears scratched.

Galen walked slowly, almost painfully, into the garage, moved over to the table and pulled the chair to sit down. The drive to the outlying area had been tiring for him. He raised his head wearily to look at Charles.

"Hi, Charles. Sorry to be troublesome, but I'm very tired. What's this news that you said you have for us?"

Nora pulled up a chair beside Galen and took his hand. "Galen, is everything all right? You look a little pale."

"Oh, I'm fine. Just a little tired is all," he smiled. "I'd just like to get this information so I can get back home to bed. I need some rest."

Landon frowned as he looked between the old man and Nora. He glanced over at Charles and saw that Charles was focused on Galen as well. Landon coughed to break the silence.

"Brad should be here any minute," said Charles as his attention was brought back to the present. "He called this morning to say he had some intelligence for us that we might find quite interesting."

"That's it?" asked Landon. "He didn't say anything more?"

Charles moved over and sat at the table across from Galen. "Nope, nothing more," he said as he turned to look at the open door.

Bob ran to the door, hesitated a moment, and then started wagging his tail.

"Looks like someone that he knows is coming," said Landon.

Nora, Landon and Charles went out to greet him when they heard Brad's car coming into the yard. He stopped abruptly and quickly pushed the door open, almost tripping and falling down as he jumped out with a canvas satchel.

"Hi, everyone," he called. "Sorry I'm late. Let's go inside."

They went back into the garage and found that Galen had nodded off to sleep in his chair. Nora rushed over to him and touched his arm. He awoke with a start, and quickly checked his surroundings. He turned to Nora and smiled.

"I guess I was more tired than I thought," he said. He looked up and saw Brad. "Ah, the messenger has arrived. Pray, my good man, illuminate us," he laughed.

The five of them sat at the table with Brad taking his seat at the head and the other four on each side looking toward him. He reached into the satchel and drew out some printouts and a map. He spread them out on the table, while the others collected around him.

"What I have here are some printouts of Grimm's communications with The Coalition in Vancouver. On a positive note, he has done what you asked him to do and it looks like they're going to respond positively. Apparently, the last thing they want is to have any criminal charges levied against the CEO of any large corporation. Apparently, that would be bad for business."

"Bad for business?" Landon asked. "I can see it would be bad for that corporation but how would it affect any others?"

Brad separated one of the printed sheets of paper from the rest and slid it across the table to Landon.

"Further down, toward the end of the page, you'll see that their concern is that if it appears that management of corporations can be held accountable for the actions of the company, they are afraid that fewer organizations would want to invest here."

Landon raised his eyes to look at Brad. "Of all the correspondence that takes place, how did you manage to get this one?"

"We have hacked into The Coalition's information system and a couple of my friends and I have been going over their documents."

"How did you manage to do that?" asked Nora. "I thought they would have the best security system available. I'm very impressed."

"There is no such thing as a system that cannot be hacked. If one geek can secure it, there's always another who could breach the security," Brad grinned.

"Does that mean that our system is vulnerable as well? Are we at any risk by having the documents that we have backed up on it?" asked Landon.

"Not really," said Brad. "At least I don't think so. The difference is that we know their database exists and where it is. They know nothing about ours. At this point their documentation indicates that they only suspect there is an organized group of people working against them; they have no real knowledge."

"I'm happy to hear that Grimm is doing the right thing," said Galen.

"We learnt something else," said Brad. "Something that involves the GroundSave Mining Corporation."

Everyone gawked at him in anticipation.

"Seven years ago an operation known as Windfall Mining was fined for polluting the water near a community over in the Northwest Territories. No criminal charges were laid, but our research indicates that three people, including one elder, died as a result of their negligence...or neglect."

"Are you saying that the management of GroundSave should have known better because of that?" asked Nora.

Brad looked up at her with no joy on his face.

"The president of the Windfall Mining was Melody Lloyd," he said quietly. "She did exactly the same thing here as she did there. This time it was Gwen and Paddy's little girl that was sacrificed to their bottom line."

Nora moved back in her chair and let her head fall backward, her eyes closed. She started shaking her head slowly.

"I don't understand how anyone could do that. I just don't understand."

Everyone in the garage was silent until Brad's enthusiastic movement forward got their attention. "There's more," he said excitedly. "We'll get into more of their data later but right now I want to tell you about the towers."

"Towers?" asked Landon.

Brad leaned forward and looked from side to side at the others as they grew more curious.

"You know about the small towers that have cropped up around Whitehorse over the years?" he asked with a mischievous grin.

"You mean the ones they started building back around 2012?" asked Nora.

Landon was immediately intrigued. "They built one by the pump house on Two Mile Hill and in Riverdale in 2012. Are those the ones you're talking about?"

"Exactly," said Brad. "You'll notice that there have been several others installed all around Whitehorse—Porter Creek, Copper Ridge and more." He set the map on the stack of papers in front of him.

Nora stretched over the table to get a better look. There were eight towers indicated between the southern city limits and the northern.

"Aren't those part of the old Northwestel system?" she asked.

"That's what everyone thought," said Brad. "As it turns out, they were used solely for the transmission of secured communication between the territorial government of the day and the federal government."

"Why would they bother with that?" Landon asked.

"Ah, there's the rub," said Galen. "Let me see if I understand this correctly. A telecommunication system was set up for the two governments who were in the process of signing agreements with China that would culminate in *The Agreement*. Back in 2012 there was still an act to enforce that allowed everyone access to any information that the government generated. The only way around the Access to Information and Protection of Privacy Act would be to circumvent the public information technology system entirely. Am I on the right track so far, Brad?"

"Precisely," Brad grinned. "There was no way for the average person to know that those transmissions ever took place. Fortunately for us, one of the servers used for that purpose was left with a connection to their main information system open. I doubt they know that connection exists."

Landon stood and moved around the table beside Brad. He leaned over to more closely examine the map. "I take it they're still using these?" he asked.

"Sure are," said Brad. "For pretty much the same purpose, except now it's The Coalition who is using it for all of their Internet and telecommunication."

Landon looked down at him. "All of their Internet and telecommunication goes through these towers?"

"Yes, every single transmission goes through these towers," beamed Brad.

Galen leaned back in his chair, a smile on his face. Nora glanced up and caught Landon's eye and couldn't help but return the grin.

Charles burst out laughing. "Finally," he said. "A vulnerable spot. A veritable Achilles' heel."

"So we could stop their exchange of information?" asked Nora. "Couldn't they just turn around and use the public system?"

"We can do better than stop them," said Brad. "We can monitor them, intercept them, and even better, we can manipulate them."

Sherry dashed from one room to the other making sure everything was spotless and in perfect shape in their home before their visitors arrived. She and Danielle had agreed to have the RCMP meet with everyone at their home for an interview and she wanted everything to be just so. Danielle sat at the kitchen table reading a book. Every so often she glanced up at Sherry and smiled.

Nora, Gwen, Matt and Galen were the first to arrive with Landon and Bob not far behind. Landon let Bob out to run around the yard. A few minutes later, Charles and Brad pulled into the driveway with Gérard's Jeep right behind them. The silent approach of a Toyota Prius announced the arrival of Stone and Kirsten.

The Frasers' living room was alive with energy and friendly banter when Sherry ran into the room. "The RCMP are here!" she exclaimed, scarcely able to contain her excitement.

She ran back to the front door to greet the two plainclothes officers, one man and one woman, and the middle-aged woman in a business suit that was with them.

"Hi," Sherry bubbled as they approached her. "Come on in. Everyone's here. Can I get you something—coffee, tea, water?"

"No, thank you, Ma'am," said the male officer as he smiled at her exuberance. "If it's all right, we'll just come in and meet everyone."

Sherry led them to the living room where two chairs waited for them. She quickly dragged another up beside them for the woman in the suit. All eyes were on them, wondering what would take place next.

"Good afternoon, everyone," said the policeman. "My name is Sgt. Bill Preston. This," he said indicating the young woman to his right, "is my partner, Cpl. Amanda King, and over here is Janet Howe. Ms. Howe is the Crown Attorney assigned to this case."

Galen and Landon looked at each other, their eyes sparkling. They turned back toward Preston, King and Howe.

Preston was already smiling as he caught their eye. "Yes, I know. We've heard it all," he chuckled. "Sgt. Preston of the RCMP and his partner King. I trust we can get past that." He smiled at the group. Cpl. King sat with a staid expression.

"Just so you know, no decision has been made to move forward with this investigation at this time," said Howe. "We are simply on a fact-finding mission and will decide what to do after we have all the information at hand."

"As you are probably aware, it was Ms. Allerton's article that first got our attention. She mentioned a mine that was located within 20 kilometres of Whitehorse and we were concerned about water quality," said Preston. "She and Stone told us that, between you, you have enough evidence to lay criminal charges. We're here to gather that material if it's still available."

Gwen described to them how, on a walk through the forest, her daughter had been poisoned by taking a drink from a stream. Dr. Archibeque confirmed that he had been the attending physician and that Keira had ingested cyanide.

Janet softly considered Gwen. "I'm so sorry for your loss," she empathized. "Please understand that the questions I'm going to ask are not because I have any doubt in what you are telling me. But in order to get this before a judge, and to obtain a conviction, we need irrefutable evidence, hard evidence. We're going to need something tangible. Our experience is that without having that, The Coalition will ensure that there is no finding of guilt."

She turned to Stone. "I understand that you have something for us?"

Stone hesitated and then looked at Kirsten. She nodded and touched his shoulder. He reached into his pocket and took out a small glass vial with the top taped down and held it up for everyone to see.

"When Kirsten and I were at the stream where Keira was poisoned, I garnered a sample of the water," he said as he turned his attention to the three newcomers. "I'm an environmental scientist so I always have tools and material with me to gather samples. You'll see a label on this file that has the date and time it was collected, as well as the location."

"Well, that's very interesting," said Cpl. King. "But it doesn't really tie anything to anybody or prove anything. We're going to need a lot more."

"I can tell you that Melody Lloyd from the GroundSave Mining Corporation assures us that the water in that stream is clear and pure," said Howe. "Her claim is that it always has been and that the mine wasn't operating at the time in question."

Gérard leaned back in his chair and crossed his arms. Distrust caused him to feel uncomfortable cooperating with any form of authority.

"I have photographs of the mining operation that was dumping the effluent down that Creek into the Fish Lake," he blurted. "They clearly show that there were no remedial measures being taken to make sure the water was clean before being released. They are all dated and stamped with the GPS location as well."

Howe took in the room slowly. "All that is really helpful...but what we need in order to tie it all together is some sort of eyewitness account that the mine was operating at the time; someone who can say that they saw employees there and that the water was being allowed to flow through a pond without settling."

Kirsten's eyes flicked over to Stone who turned his head slightly to catch Landon's attention. Landon gave them a stoic look. They were all wondering if this visit was a fishing expedition to learn who had infiltrated the mine site in order to lay those charges.

"Whatever you want," Landon said softly. "I understand either way."

Stone turned toward Kirsten's eyes, searching for an answer. She closed her lids gently, then slowly lifted them and, with a resigned look on her face, she nodded.

Janet Howe was perplexed as she watched the short exchange. "Is one of you going to tell me what's going on?" she asked.

Stone took a deep breath and began telling her about the night they had slipped past the guards into the mining compound. Both Landon and Kirsten added information as the story unfolded. The two RCMP officers and Howe listened attentively.

When they were done telling the story, Howe sat back in her chair and rolled her eyes toward the ceiling. Then she turned to Sgt. Preston. "Is there anything more you would like to ask?"

Preston thought for a few seconds and then shook his head no. Howe then turned to Cpl. King who shook her head no as well.

"Thank you, folks," she said. "We'll take all of this under advisement and we'll let you know what we decide to do in due course."

"It's not the first time that bitch has poisoned people!" snapped Danielle. Her sudden outburst brought everyone's attention to her. "Some people died in the Northwest Territories because of her and her damned mining," she continued as she observed the others in the room. "It looks like she's going to get away with it this time too." She turned angrily to Preston, King and Howe. "When are you guys ever going to do anything?"

Preston sat patiently waiting for a few seconds to pass.

"Ms. Fraser, is it?" he said. "I can assure you that if we can gather enough evidence to lay charges and have them stick, in this case, that is exactly what will be done."

He took his time looking very slowly around the room, catching the eye of each of the individuals in front of him, one at a time.

"The N.W.T. incident you mentioned is not a matter of public knowledge as there were never any charges laid so no files exist on it. Tell me, how do you know about it?"

"Rumour," interjected Galen. "Strictly rumours that we've heard over the past little while. Apparently, they were truer than some of us thought." His eyes held steady with the policeman's.

Sgt. Preston frowned slightly, then relaxed and smiled. "Then I guess we're done here for now," he said.

The three visitors thanked everyone for their time and promised to get back to them with their decision as soon as it was made. Sherry showed them to the door and thanked them for coming. A moment later, they backed out of the driveway and drove up the street.

When Sherry returned to the living room she saw a very agitated Gwen standing behind her chair. Tears formed in Gwen's eyes.

"She's done it before?" she asked. "She's done it before and got away with it so now my little Keira is gone. That's just not right. It's just not right."

Nora walked over to her and took her in her arms.

Later that day, Chong demanded a meeting with Preston, King and Howe. They arrived at the Windsor Boardroom of the old Edgewater Hotel to find both Chong and Poste waiting for them. As they walked in the room, Preston noted that Chong, while appearing quite calm, was fidgeting with keys in his pocket. Poste was obviously very nervous.

Norm Hamilton

"Come in, sit," said Chong as he motioned with both hands to the chairs around the huge mahogany table. "I am very pleased that you could come."

Poste slid the doors to the meeting room closed and remained standing.

The Crown Attorney quietly sat down and followed Chong with her eyes. Sgt. Preston took a seat beside her while Cpl. King moved to a chair against the wall where she could observe everyone in the room.

"I have asked you here so we can clear up misunderstandings that brought you here," said Chong. "I trust when you leave here today there will be no need for you to return."

"We're all ears," said Preston. "Please, carry on."

"As we are all aware," began Chong, "it is important that The Coalition not be dragged into any controversy. Our people at The Capitol would be very unhappy if that were to happen. They have given me the authority to do what is necessary to make sure that they're not embarrassed by this incident."

Preston cocked his head toward Chong. "And what is it you're supposed to do?" he asked. "We're here to see if there has been a criminal offence. We will gather information, and evidence if there is any, and we will proceed in an appropriate manner from there."

"Our militia," Chong indicated toward Poste, "has investigated this already and we have concluded that it is a simple matter to deal with, purely an accident. We will make sure the company gets a fine and is reprimanded. I'm sorry your time has been wasted."

The silence that followed was broken when Howe cleared her throat. She rolled her eyes toward Chong. "We will decide whether an investigation is required or not.

208

Certainly, your militia is not going to decide for us what is and what isn't necessary."

"Maybe I'm not making myself clear," retorted Chong. "The Coalition has said they want it dealt with the way I said we would deal with it. That means your work here is done."

Howe and Preston rose in unison. At the same time, Cpl. King moved toward the door, startling Poste. Howe looked directly into Chong's eyes with an ironic grin.

"Thank you for your time and for your suggestion. We'll give it all due consideration."

With that, she turned and walked through the door that King was holding open. The two RCMP members followed.

When they got to the sidewalk, she turned to the two officers. "Now, there's a guarantee that there's more going on than meets the eye. I was a little hesitant until now; we are definitely opening a full-fledged criminal investigation into the death of that little girl."

As they walked toward their car, Janet Howe ruminated on the day seven years prior when her grandfather succumbed to cyanide poisoning in the hospital in Yellowknife.

Chapter 19

Poste had to run a couple of steps every few strides in an attempt to keep up with Chong as he charged across the parking lot toward the riverfront building housing Lloyd's office. Chong was moving like a man possessed— his eyes straight ahead, focused only on the entrance. He shoved open the door and kicked it to the side.

In his haste to stay close to Chong, Poste tried to slide through the door as it swung shut. The door handle caught on the pocket of his trench coat, stopping his upper body dead; his feet pulled out from underneath him and he fell flat on his back. By then, Chong was standing at the elevator button trying to get the car to hurry up. Poste scrambled to his feet and extricated himself from the door. He ran to the elevator and managed to squeeze through the doors just before they closed. They rode to the third floor in silence. The doors slid open and they strode toward Melody Lloyd's office.

Tom Alexander fidgeted in his chair as he stared out over the vehicles in the back. He'd seen them enter the building and was not looking forward to the meeting in Lloyd's office. Chong's attitude and behaviour scared him and knowing that Poste would do anything he was told was an even bigger concern. He reached down and grabbed the bottle of Jack Daniels from the lower desk drawer. He stared through glazed eyes as he unscrewed the top, and then picked up a glass.

The glass hit the desk with a *thunk* as he slammed it back down. Tipping the bottle of whiskey back, he swallowed hard twice. His eyes were still watering when he screwed the top back on and then turned and headed for the door.

Chong had insinuated himself into Lloyd's leather-covered chair behind the large desk as soon as she let them into her office. Poste was standing off to one side, unsure what to do with himself.

"Sit down," Chong snarled to no one in particular.

Alexander hesitated and then rushed to be at Lloyd's side after she dragged a seat to the front of the desk. The late afternoon sunlight reflected off the cut-banks of the river through the glass wall behind them. Poste drew a chair up beside the desk near Chong.

"We have to stop those fools now," said Chong. "They have the RCMP and the damn Crown Attorney's office looking at things now."

"But, that Crown Attorney lady said she was going to consider what you said," said Poste.

Chong was revolted. "You fool," he said. "She said she would give it 'all due consideration.' When a lawyer uses the words 'all due' it's the same as saying 'none'. It's like when they stand in court feeling disdain for the other lawyer—they will refute the former's statement by beginning with 'with all due respect to my learned friend.' She simply told us that she wasn't going to pay any attention to what we said."

"Can they do that?" asked Alexander. "Don't they have to do what you tell them?"

"No. Criminal matters are the one area that The Coalition has stayed away from, "Chong chided. "It would be an international public relations nightmare if they tried to take over countries' criminal courts as well. This is something we're going to have to deal with ourselves."

He turned to Poste.

"You can start with that old man from the Town Hall Meeting. Make him fold and the rest will follow."

"I can deal with that old prick," squealed Post. "I'll teach him for interfering with us at that damn meeting."

"No one's going to get hurt now," Alexander demanded. "Right?"

Chong squinted directly at Alexander. "It's entirely up to them. They can back off...or not."

Melody Lloyd sat strangely silent, her reticence speaking volumes.

Nora made coffee while Landon and Galen sat in the living room of Galen's small apartment. They had come over to see how Galen was doing as Nora was concerned because of his constant drowsiness at the last meeting. They found him asleep in his chair, but happy to see them once he woke. The only other furnishings in his apartment were a couch and a table with two chairs, and a bed in the bedroom.

Galen examined the floor and then looked over at Landon. "Where's Bob?" he asked. "I don't think I've ever seen you without him."

"He hurt his leg during a run through the bush yesterday, a nasty cut. The vet said to leave him overnight to make sure it didn't get infected."

"I'm sure he's going to be okay," said Galen. "Please, find yourself a seat."

"It's been a very busy few weeks," said Landon as he accepted a coffee from Nora and sat at the table. "How are you holding up?" he asked Galen.

"As good as an old man can," laughed Galen.

Nora handed him a steaming mug. "I've been worried about you," she said. "You've been going steady for a long time. Maybe you shouldn't be a part of this."

Galen peered over the rim of his glasses and smiled at her. "At my age it's good to be a part of anything. I wouldn't change what we're doing for the world."

He turned back to Landon.

"It's a difficult predicament we find ourselves in. People have gone from ignoring what's going on around them to wanting to put a stop to everything. The reality is you cannot stop everything. The earthquake really shook people up, no pun intended," he said. "People have been living in denial for so long that having reality thrust on them as harshly as that has been quite a shock. I expect everything will even out over time."

Nora sat on the end of the sofa near her two friends, holding her cup in both hands. She nodded her head slightly.

"That's true, we humans tend to react to something like that in a drastic fashion and then slowly return to our previous position because it is what we're used to and what feels comfortable. Right now people are demanding that all mining and oil and gas work be forced to stop. One group has gone as far as lobbying the federal government."

Galen smiled at the reference. "They can lobby all they want," he said. "The reality is that exploration and extraction of mineral and gas resources are essential realities. Everything we have is made from, or relies on those resources so we cannot just stop mining and oil and gas companies from doing their work. What we need is balance. If we go too far one way or the other there are problems. When our focus is only on environment we have a low economy; if we focus entirely on business, we destroy the environment. Balance is paramount—we need the environment to survive but we also need to have healthy enterprise operating. During this century we have forgotten to maintain that equilibrium. Equanimity in thought is what we seek."

Nora and Landon nodded in agreement. The three of them discussed the affairs of the day for an hour or so before Galen suggested they go for a walk. They grabbed their jackets and took Landon's truck over to the Rotary Centennial Bridge. As they stepped out of the pickup, a black Dodge four-wheel-drive with darkened windows pulled up behind them.

Two of the darkly dressed militia pulled themselves out of the front of the truck. Poste emerged from the back seat and started to walk toward Landon's truck with the other two close behind. He checked the truck bed and then went to the driver's window and looked in the cab.

"No dog," he grinned at the others. They separated as he walked between them to go around the back of the truck and started walking directly toward Galen.

"Come on, old man, we're taking you in for questioning," he commanded. Galen retreated toward the front of the vehicle. Landon stepped in front of Galen as Nora stepped a couple of meters to the side.

"Don't make this difficult," Poste snarled. "We're taking him and there's nothing you can do about it."

"He's not going anywhere with you," Landon asserted. "The best bet would be for you boys to get back in your car and leave."

Poste laughed ironically, motioning to his henchmen with his hands. "Do you really think you can stop the three of us by yourself?"

"He's not alone," said Nora easily. "Like he said, nobody's going with you."

Poste sized up the situation and then ordered his two henchmen to jump Landon as he moved in to deal with Galen. He ignored Nora entirely.

Landon's 44 Magnum roared and a scream of agony was heard as one of the goons went down clutching his right thigh. As the revolver started to turn toward the second man, a nightstick came down on his wrist with a sickening crash. He turned to face his foe, his arm shattered. The man moved forward and swung the nightstick again. Landon raised his arm to block it. Then the other end of it was brought up under his arm connecting with his jaw. His head flew back and the nightstick was delivered butt first into his gut, knocking the wind out of him. He slumped to his knees, head down, completely vulnerable.

Nearby, Nora had stepped between Poste and Galen, infuriating the militia director. Poste circled around Nora as she casually turned on her feet to face him. He feinted toward her a couple of times in an attempt to scare her. She didn't flinch.

This is going to be easy, he thought. *She doesn't even know enough to move when I go to attack her.* He slid the nightstick from his belt and stood with his feet apart facing her.

"Run, bitch!" he screamed as he lunged toward her with his baton above his head.

Nora moved directly toward him, catching him by surprise. When she was a meter away she stepped sideways and brought one knee toward her chest. As he continued to move forward her leg rapidly extended with her heel connecting directly to his lower sternum. His eyes bulged

215

out and a whooshing sound escaped his lips. He stood, rattled and confused, as his weapon dropped to the ground. Nora took another step forward and planted her knuckles directly into his throat. Then she spun rapidly as one foot rose from ground level and collided with the side of his face. Poste's eyes rolled back in his head as he crumpled to the ground. She whirled around to find Landon.

Landon was on the ground protecting his head with his hands as the militia man kept swinging the heavy wooden pole. The man glanced over to see Nora standing beside the fallen Poste and then turned back to Landon. He raised his stick high over his head to deliver the final blow.

There was a loud explosion and the nightstick shattered in his hands. He cried out in pain as his hands started bleeding profusely. He pivoted, snarling, in the direction of the sound to see Galen standing beside the pickup with Landon's Winchester pulled to his shoulder. The fight dropped from the militia man.

"Pick him up and get out of here," Galen said quietly as he pointed the rifle barrel briefly at Poste. Out of the corner of his eye he saw another vehicle approaching. He swung the rifle over so it faced the rental truck that drove up and parked beside the militia vehicle.

Galen counted three people in the truck as it sat with no apparent activity. Nora rushed to help Landon to his feet and then they moved to the old Chevy beside Galen. They watched with curiosity while the rented vehicle continued to sit motionless as the militia members dragged Poste to their vehicle and backed out to spin away toward town.

When the dust died down, the doors of the rental truck opened and Sgt. Preston, Cpl. King, and Janet Howe stepped out. Galen lowered the rifle, then turned and laid it on the pickup seat.

"It looks like you're having an interesting day," said Preston as they moved toward the pickup. "Is there anything we can do to help?"

Landon eyed them warily, watching closely as they approached.

"I think we're okay," he offered, with a slight frown on his face.

"You're absolutely sure?" asked Howe. "It kind of looks like you were assaulted. You know, contrary to popular belief, those fools from the militia have no more legal authority than any other security guard. People just think they do."

Preston turned to Galen. "As an example, they do not have the authority to detain anyone unless there is a court order." He continued to look calmly at Galen. "If they were to do that, it could result in criminal charges." He smiled broadly.

Galen returned the smile. "I think we're okay for the moment but you and I may want to have a little chat later on."

Preston glanced down at Landon's injured arm. "It looks like you should go over and get that wrist looked at," he smiled.

He stepped in close to the three of them. "That was pretty impressive, the way the three of you handled yourselves," he whispered softly. "It's too bad we didn't get here a moment earlier."

He stepped back and glanced toward Howe and King.

"I guess we'll just carry on with our Millennium Trail walk then."

They turned to wave as they headed across the foot bridge.

Landon turned to Nora with a quizzical look on his face. "Where did you learn to do that?" he asked. "I've never seen anyone defend themselves like that before. It was amazing."

Nora gently cupped Landon's elbow in one hand and guided his wrist upward with the other.

"Keep your arm elevated so that it doesn't swell anymore. It will also help with the pain," she said. She smiled at the questioning look he was giving her. "I studied the martial arts for a number of years when I was younger," she said. "I never thought I would ever need it to defend myself. At the time I just did it for the exercise."

Galen laughed out loud. "You should've seen the look on Poste's face when you knocked the wind out of him. When I think about it now, I can't help but laugh."

Nora examined the side of Landon's face. "Well, now, that's going to leave a mark," she said. "We better get you over to see Matt."

Landon winced as they clambered into the truck, with Nora behind the wheel. "We really have to put a stop to those bullies. And we have to do it now," he said.

The rear tires threw some gravel as Nora sped out of the parking lot. Three sets of eyes watched from a quiet spot on the Millennium Trail as they departed.

"It looks like we're going to have all the help we need to make the charges stick," said Howe to the two plainclothes officers with her. "Let's go do some paperwork and then make some arrests."

Chapter 20

The laughter was infectious as Galen described the scuffle between Nora and Poste. For her part, Nora shyly minimized her role. Bob gaily dashed to and fro from one person to another in his exuberance to see them all. Landon had turned his cabin over to Nora, Danielle and Sherry so they could prepare dinner. Galen had called everyone together at Landon's place for an afternoon of friendship and relaxation. He said the large camouflage tent could serve well as a place to party as well as it did a place to meet.

Landon smiled as he considered his new friends. Gérard, Charles and Matt were at one table with a deck of cards between them while Kirsten and Stone were engrossed in some electronic gadget that Brad had arrived with. It all reminded him of the time before *The Agreement*.

"Has anyone seen Gwen lately?" he asked the group.

"The last I heard she and Paddy had started a counselling program to help them deal with everything," said Nora as she stepped out of the cabin and moved up beside him. "I sure hope it works for them. They're such a nice couple."

Galen came into the tent and sat at the table with Charles and the other two men. He signalled to Landon and Nora to come and sit with them. Danielle and Sherry came out of the cabin and brought a bowl of fruit punch into the enclosure. They ladled it into mugs and distributed the sweet drink to everyone.

"A toast to change," said Galen. "To a return to sanity."

"To change! To sanity!" they all shouted amidst laughter and the clinking together of mugs.

"You really think they're going to go ahead and lay criminal charges?" Charles asked Galen as the mirth passed. "It seems like forever since anything was done when a resource company destroyed the environment."

"These two RCMP and the Crown Attorney that's with them appear to be quite focused in their intent," said Galen. "It looks to me like they take their work very seriously. If I read them correctly, we will see some arrests made before the week is out."

"Oh, that would be so exciting," squealed Sherry. "Finally, we get some justice."

"Arrests don't necessarily mean convictions," said Charles as he raised his eyebrows.

"But, they're certainly a good start," countered Landon. "Yup, they are an excellent start."

Danielle turned to face the table where the older group of her friends sat.

"What about the militia?" she asked. "You said that Ms. Howe told you they have no more authority than a security guard. They've been going around Whitehorse bullying people and forcing their way onto properties to enforce The Coalition's rules. How can they do that if they don't have any authority?"

"They have the authority to enforce those rules," said Landon. "But the only way they're supposed to enforce them is by writing tickets or charging people and taking them to court."

"Then why do they need to be armed and carrying nightsticks?" Danielle asked.

"They don't," said Landon. "If you remember, four years ago when the RCMP contract ended and the militia arrived, they had none of that. It wasn't until Poste took over as Director that we started to have any real problems with them. And now that Chong is here, well, it's gotten way out of hand."

Nora picked up her mug and sipped at its fruity contents. "Do you think now that the RCMP are here that it'll make a difference?" she asked. "Do you think there will be any change?"

"Probably not," said Galen. "Unless they're planning on charging Poste or Chong as well."

"I doubt we'd ever see that happen," said Charles. "Trying to get someone convicted that is being backed by The Capitol would be next to impossible. We'll have to look for other ways to deal with them. In the meantime let's celebrate the successes that we do have."

Nora raised her eyes and looked around. "It's a sad celebration though. A little girl was sacrificed for it to happen. It makes the victory so bittersweet." She paused a moment, and then her face broke into a smile. "But this is a happier time, so let's enjoy it."

Danielle, Sherry and Nora left the tent to return to the cabin. Landon smiled as he watched them bustling around, finishing the meal preparations. He turned to look across the table and ask Galen a question, but found him slumped in his chair.

"Galen?" he said. "Hey, Galen!" he repeated louder.

Landon's insistence prompted Charles, who was sitting beside Galen, to reach over and shake his friend gently, calling his name. There was no response. Brad jumped up and ran into the cabin and brought Nora back. Galen's eyes opened and he sat erect as she arrived.

She checked his eyes. One pupil appeared larger than the other and he seemed somewhat confused. "Galen, can you hear me?" she asked.

His words were slurred as he tried to answer her. He kept looking around at everyone, mumbling something about everything being blurry.

"I have a terrible headache," he finally managed to say.

"It's okay. We're going to look after things," she said as she motioned for Matt to come over. "You sit in the car with him and I'll drive us to the hospital," she said to Matt. She turned back to Galen. "Matt's going to look after you and we're going to take you to the hospital, do you understand that?"

Galen nodded slowly and Nora ran to her car. Matt and Charles carried Galen and laid him on his side in the back of the station wagon. Matt crawled in with him and pulled the door shut. The Subaru clawed at the gravel with all four tires as Nora sped out of the yard. The rest of them could do nothing more than watch as they disappeared from sight.

Nora phoned Landon about two hours later.

"Tell everyone that Galen had a small stroke but seems to be doing well," she said. "Matt said that he stayed conscious for the whole trip into the hospital and that he seems to be in good spirits."

"Man, that's good to hear. We've been pretty scared for him. I'll give everyone the good news."

"There's one more thing, totally unrelated," Nora said with hesitation.

"Okay, what is the other thing?" Landon wasn't sure if he wanted to hear anything more.

"Gwen called. She said that when she told Paddy that Melody Lloyd was running a mine in the Northwest Territories that poisoned people, he got very angry. She tried to calm him down but in the end he took off."

"Did she say where he was going?"

"Only that he said something about 'making it right.' That was it. He said he was going to make it right."

"So, we have no idea where he went or what he's doing?"

"Nothing at all. No idea."

"I'll see what we can do. You stay with Galen and I'll talk to everyone here. I'll try to keep you up-to-date."

He went back in the tent and called everyone together to tell them the news about Galen...and about Paddy. After explaining the situation he suggested that they split up into as many vehicles as possible and see if they could locate Paddy. They talked about someone going to the GroundSave Mining site but decided to limit their search to around the City of Whitehorse because they didn't know how to get to the mine by road. They each chose a different subdivision. Landon took the downtown core.

Landon opened the pickup door and called Bob. The other four vehicles were already pulling out of the yard and rushing toward town. He looked down at the sling on his arm and then reached up with his other hand and undid the knots holding it in place. He glanced over at Bob and let out a deep sigh as he reached toward the stick shift, cast and all.

A myriad of questions rushed through Landon's mind as he raced toward Whitehorse. *What the hell is he up to? Where would he go? What's he going to do?*

A short time later, Landon was racing up 2nd Avenue when he glanced toward the river and saw Paddy's

223

rusting Kia Sportage sitting crossways of some parking spots near the waterfront, close to what used to be the Shipyards Park. He guided his pickup into the lot to have a look.

Melody Lloyd had been pacing in her office for over an hour. *Why were the R.C.M.P in Whitehorse*, she wondered. *Do they have enough evidence to lay any charges?* She was waiting for Chong, Alexander, and Poste to come for a meeting. She grabbed the glass of brandy she'd poured earlier and threw it back.

That fucking Alexander will be no help, she thought. *Goddamn chicken-shit, yes-man. I never should have hired the son of a bitch. Damn, where the hell is he?*

Her office door opened and he walked in, appearing unsteady on his feet.

"Where the hell have you been?" she snapped.

"Uh, in my office reviewing files to make sure we got everything covered," he slurred.

"Oh, shit," she said, shaking her head. "You've been sitting down there drinking all day. Great! You're going to be absolutely useless."

He turned and walked over and flopped down sloppily into a chair. "I think we're screwed, Melody," he said. "I just have the feeling that we're not going to get any backup."

Lloyd walked over to his chair and sneered down at him.

"That's why we're here. We're going to make sure that Chong looks after us." She glanced at her watch as she turned to look out the window over the river. "Where the hell is he? He was supposed to be here 20 minutes ago. Shit, he probably told that idiot Poste."

224

They both turned toward the door as Chong pushed it open and walked into the room. He threw his overcoat onto a chair as he strode through the room, once again, to take over Lloyd's chair behind the desk.

"Poste will be here in a minute," he said. "In the meantime why don't you pull up some chairs and have a seat in front of the desk where I can see you better." His eyes narrowed even further. "I don't know what you expect, but there's only so much that I can do."

"But, you have to make sure we're safe," said Alexander. "You have to look after us."

Chong frowned at him, and then turned to Lloyd. "What is he talking about?"

"Everything we've done is because of *The Agreement*. So we think you need to make sure that no charges are pressed."

"*The Agreement* doesn't permit criminal activity," Chong said, shaking his head. "It's only supposed to protect the income for resource corporations. If you've done something beyond that you're on your own."

Alexander rolled his eyes and then closed them as he slumped even further into his chair, his arms hanging limply at his sides.

Lloyd glared fiercely at Chong. "You son of a bitch! You're going to sell us out, aren't you?"

Chong sat passively, not responding to her. He turned his head toward the door as Poste walked in. The three of them were shocked to see the massive bruising on the side of his face.

"What happened to you?" Chong asked.

"You told me to get the old man—" Poste began.

"An old man did that to you?"

"No, there were others with him. That woman, Nora—"

"You let an old woman beat the shit out of you?" Chong said disgustedly. "You? The Director of the Militia here and you get taken down by an old woman? Didn't you have anyone with you?"

"I had two men with me but they got the drop on us with the rifle before we could get the old man," Poste whined. "I had it under control until then," he added, keeping his eyes averted.

Chong was shaking his head when the office door burst open and Paddy Doyle stepped in. He moved halfway into the office and stood, breathing heavily, and glared at the four occupants of the room. Chong was seated behind the desk with Lloyd and Alexander in front of him like two children in the principal's office. Poste was standing at the side of the desk gingerly touching his damaged face.

"By Jesus," he said. "I never thought when I followed that little prick here that I'd have all four of you in one room. This must be my lucky day."

Chong stood up behind the desk and started to raise his voice.

"Sit down and shut up!" said Paddy. "None of you have anything to say that I want to hear."

Chong frowned at Poste. "Get him out of here," he ordered.

Poste took one step forward, and then froze in his tracks.

Lloyd and Alexander looked into Poste's wide eyes and then turned around to see what had startled him. Paddy was standing with his coat open, displaying the packs of explosives that he had strapped to his body, his breath coming in deeper, shorter gasps.

226

"I told Gwen that I was going to make it right," he said. He turned to Alexander. "You lied to me. You said it was all an accident, a mistake. You just didn't care."

He scowled directly at Melody Lloyd. "You knew exactly what you were doing, and the chances you were taking. But you didn't think people's lives mattered."

His eyes closed briefly as he took a deep breath.

He glanced down at the switch in his hand, and then returned his gaze to his hostages. Alexander and Lloyd began pleading with him. Poste stood with his eyes wide open as the front of his pants darkened and his boot filled with the warm liquid he could no longer retain. Only Chong had regained his composure.

Paddy heard a slight noise behind him. His fingers tightened on the switch, then he heard a familiar voice call his name quietly.

"Paddy. Paddy, it's okay. Gwen wants you to come home."

He turned his head enough to see Landon standing just inside the office door with Bob standing by his side.

"Get out of here," said Paddy. "This has nothing to do with you. There's no need for you to get hurt too."

"Gwen asked me to come and get you," Landon said softly.

"They think they're going to get away with murdering our little girl," said Paddy. "I'm going to make sure they don't." He turned his eyes toward the other four and then spoke over his shoulder to Landon.

"Please go. I don't want you to get hurt."

"Paddy, we talked to the RCMP and the Crown Attorney. They are going to lay criminal charges. There's enough evidence to put those responsible away for lifetime."

Tom Alexander burst into tears. Lloyd fainted in her chair.

Paddy glanced back and noticed Landon's cast and bruised face.

"He do that to you?" he asked, nodding toward Poste.

"Are you kidding? No, his goons did."

"Then who did that?" Paddy asked, pointing to Poste's face.

"Nora."

"Nora? Really? Nora?" Paddy stood silent for a moment and then started to laugh. He looked over at Landon. "You sure the RCMP is going to charge them?"

"As sure as I can be."

Paddy took another deep breath.

"God, I hope you're right," he said as he released his grip on the switch connected to the explosives.

Poste started to run toward the door in an effort to escape. He was met by a growl and a large set of teeth. Bob held fast at the door as Poste slunk back toward the desk.

Landon glanced back into the hallway and then stepped to the side as Sgt. Preston and Cpl. King made their way into the office.

"It looks like everything is well in hand here," said Preston. "Thanks for the call," he added as he glanced over at Landon.

"No problem," said Landon.

"We'll take it from here," said Preston. "You and your friend are free to go."

"But, he's got a bunch of explosives!" shouted Chong.

Paddy turned toward the two officers and began buttoning up his coat. He looked at them questioningly.

"There's no law against transporting explosives," said Preston. "No law at all."

Landon put his arm over Paddy's shoulder as they walked down the hallway. He called to Bob who was still snarling at Poste. Bob ran through the door with his tail wagging.

They reached the elevator and pushed the button. As they stood waiting, they heard Cpl. King's muffled voice. "Melody Lloyd, you are being charged in the death of Keira Doyle—"

The elevator arrived and they stepped in.

When they reached the Kia, Landon helped Paddy free himself from the explosives. As the last of them was removed, they saw Nora's car coming toward them. She ground to a halt and Gwen jumped out of the passenger door and ran to Paddy. She threw her arms around him and began to cry.

"I thought I was going to lose you too," she sobbed. "I couldn't stand that."

"I'm so sorry. I didn't know what else to do," Paddy said as the tears streamed down his face.

Nora moved over beside Landon and slipped her arm around his waist. They watched as their friends hugged and kissed each other. Landon draped his arm over her shoulder as she laid her head against him.

They both glanced up at the top floor of the building where the arrests were being made and then strolled toward their vehicles.

Chapter 21

Wolfgang Grimm walked past Mahalia and into his office. He sat on the edge of the large chair facing the glossy, teak desk and pressed his thumb over the recognition pad to initiate the holographic screen of his computer system. Mahalia rose and followed as far as the door.

She smiled as she watched him organize the material he would need for his commentary to The Coalition. He always was at his best when under pressure, she thought. She admired his confidence and his proficiency.

She turned at the sound of the doors of the elevator in the hallway sliding open. Her demeanour chilled as Sam Chong stepped out. Joseph Poste and Tom Alexander scuttled behind him, almost colliding with him when he stopped in the hallway. Chong stepped forward, swung the glass door of the office open, and marched into the reception area.

Mahalia quietly closed the oak door to the inner office and returned to her desk where she stood facing the three unwelcome visitors.

"We came to see Grimm," Chong mumbled.

Mahalia smiled sweetly. "I'm afraid he's very busy at the moment. Perhaps you could make an appointment for another time?"

"There's no time for that," Chong protested. "We need to see him right away."

"Have a seat and I'll see if he can make time for you," she purred, motioning towards the settee. Poste and Alexander sat, and then jumped up to make room for

Chong. Mahalia chuckled as she slid into the inner office, closing the door behind her.

Grimm's eyebrows raised as his eyes turned towards her. "Yes, Mahalia?"

"Vice President Chong is here to see you, Wolfgang. He brought Joseph Poste and Mr. Alexander with him. He's quite insistent on seeing you right away."

Grimm switched off the screen in front of him and pushed his chair backwards. "I guess I'm going to have to deal with it sometime," he said, thinking of the previous week's fiasco at Melody Lloyd's office and the pending charges for her and Poste. "Now is as good a time as any. Have them wait for 30 minutes and then show them in, please. I'll keep myself occupied in the meantime."

Mahalia's eyes sparkled as she delivered the message to Chong and his cohorts. Then, after a half-hour of watching them fidget and fuss, she escorted them into Grimm's office, closing the door behind them. Chong headed straight for the glass-enclosed conference room.

"Sit here," Grimm scolded as he motioned towards the chairs in front of his desk. "There's no need for the conference room."

Chong's upper lip curled and his fiery eyes narrowed as he stormed to the middle of three chairs. Poste scurried to sit on Chong's left while Alexander lowered himself into the seat on his right.

"What can I do for you?" asked Grimm.

"You know damn well why we're here," spat Chong. "We need to get this mess under control. And we need to do it now."

Grimm eased back in his chair, his elbows resting on the arms, his fingers interlaced in front of him. "I believe I know the concerns and fears that brought you here, but I am unclear as to what you expect me to do about them."

Poste leapt from his chair and leaned over the desk. "You have to do something! They want to charge me with murder! You have to—"

"Sit down, Mr. Poste," Grimm commanded as he stared into Poste's eyes. "Sit down."

Poste slunk back into his seat, defeated.

Chong shook his head at Poste and then returned his attention to Grimm. "You have to get The Coalition to send somebody here to look after this mess before it gets completely out of hand."

"It's already completely out of hand, you fool," said Grimm quietly. "Remember, you were sent here to make everything right, and what we have now is the result. I don't think you're in a position to be demanding or try to control anything. Your best bet would be to let me do my job and deal with things as best they can be dealt with.

"And as for you, Mr. Alexander," he continued, eyeballing the man to his left, "I fail to understand why you are associating with the likes of these two. My advice to you is to collect your things and move somewhere quiet." Tom Alexander did not respond; he just sat with his eyes turned to the floor.

"Mr. Poste," he went on, causing Josef Poste to stiffen in his chair. "The Coalition will decide whether they want to have anything to do with you or not. It is beyond my control. I can tell you that I do not support you in any way.

"Gentlemen, my mission is to protect the reputation and public relations of The Coalition. I assure you, my job will get done. The public's perception of The Coalition

232

takes precedence over any of your paltry issues; hence, The Coalition's needs come before yours.

"The Coalition will be here, and be in control, for a long time yet to come. I intend to see that nothing gets in its way."

Grimm stood and then sauntered to the heavy oak door leading out of his office. He drew the door open and with a slight nod of his head stated, "There is nothing more to discuss. Please leave."

He smiled at Mahalia as they left, then returned to his desk and reinstated the holographic screen. After staring at the blank screen for a few moments, he began, "Mr. President, the following are my recommendations for dealing with the incidents in Yukon. As you know, it is paramount that The Coalition and the business interests of its members be protected. These proposals are intended to do just that…"

The satisfying crunch of dried leaves underfoot portended the onset of winter. Charles smiled as he looked around his yard. He believed that it was safe, for the time being, to have his friends come to celebrate Galen's 86th birthday. Several vehicles were already in the yard and the garage hummed with the voices and activity of those inside. Landon walked through the door with Bob trotting behind him.

"Any idea when Nora and Galen are coming?" Charles asked.

"They should be here any time now," said Landon. "Galen's a little slower getting around these days, but he's pretty excited about meeting with everyone again."

"He's quite the character," said Charles. "I hope I can be as sharp as he is when I'm his age."

Landon peered over Charles's shoulder as a small Toyota came in the drive. Nora's Subaru was following directly behind.

"It looks like Kirsten and Stone made it as well," said Landon. "Galen will be happy about that."

Galen slowly emerged from Nora's car, using the door to pull himself up as he steadied himself with his cane. When he felt stable he rested the walking stick against his hip and raised a hand in greeting. As he got closer, Landon noticed that his smile was off-kilter and that the left side of his face sagged slightly lower than the right. When he got to the men, he shifted the cane from his right hand to the slowly grasping fingers of his left and then reached out in greeting.

"So glad you could make it," said Charles.

"Wouldn't miss it for the world," said Galen. "Besides, Nora was at my place pushing me out the door." He gave a crooked smile.

"Well, let's go inside," said Charles. He grinned at Kirsten and Stone. "Nice to see you again. Come on in."

They walked into the garage and everyone began singing the old refrain, "For He's a Jolly Good Fellow." Galen blushed as he received the accolades from his friends. Nora guided him to his usual seat. Nora and Landon, Gérard, Charles, Brad, Matt, Danielle and Sherry, Kirsten and Stone pulled their chairs close to the table as their chatter continued. Bob lay contentedly by the door.

Galen caught Kirsten's attention. "I understand congratulations are in order," he grinned at her.

Kirsten flushed and turned her eyes downward.

Galen addressed the room. "Kirsten has been nominated for the prestigious Canadian National Award for Investigative Journalism," he began as his eyes connected with hers again. "Apparently, someone was impressed with your tenacity and ability."

"Yes, I've been very lucky."

Stone watched her and waited a few seconds. He sat up straight and looked around the room. "There's been one more thing that's happened that you might be interested in," he began. "She also wrote a story about the way the militia was treating people in this part of the country. Part of that was a report on the unfortunate demise of Ron Jerome..."

Everyone's eyes turned to Kirsten.

"The little bit that witnesses were able to tell me," she began, "showed that he was taken out of The People's Pub by Director Poste and two other militia. That was the last time anyone saw him alive. I described the way the militia are dressed here and I guess the image of the long trench coats caught someone's attention. It turns out this kind of behaviour has been spreading throughout the whole country.

"Cpl. King and Sgt. Preston confiscated Poste's coat and had some forensic work done on it. It turns out that there were traces of Ron Jerome's blood on it. When they were interrogating him he folded like a piece of origami and named his accomplices, and all three have now been charged with first-degree murder."

Galen smiled gently at her for a moment. "It's amazing how effective quality journalism can be for society," he said. "Thank God there was a publication that was not being controlled by conglomerates that printed your piece."

The chitchat among the friends started again as Galen sat back in his chair with both hands resting on his walking stick.

Nora went out to her car and returned with a huge birthday cake. After Galen blew out the number-shaped candles, she cut slices for everyone. Sherry added a dollop of ice cream to each plate as they were passed around. Each voiced their congratulations to him, as well as their appreciation.

Everyone's attention was drawn toward the doorway as it was darkened by two bodies that stood on its threshold.

"Come in. Come in," Nora said as she rushed with reaching arms to greet Gwen and Paddy. "Come and have a seat." She turned to the table and introduced them to those who didn't know them. They sat at the table as Sherry delivered large pieces of cake and ice cream to them.

Galen considered everyone in the room with admiration and gratitude.

"Speech, speech," said Landon as he smiled at Galen.

Galen's eyes were turned down toward the table for a moment, and then raised to the room.

"Thank you all for coming to share this day with me," Galen said quietly. "But more importantly, I'd like to tell you how pleased I am that we have all come together in the single cause of creating positive change."

He looked directly at Gwen and Paddy.

"I haven't had a chance to tell you this," he began, "but I am so very sorry for your loss and I fully understand that no success that we have managed could ever remove your pain. The heartbreak of losing a child can never be mended."

He brought his attention to the rest of the room again.

236

"Your efforts have made it possible, not only for the RCMP to do their job and lay the charges in this case, but a precedent has been set now that, hopefully, will cause a change in the way things are done. As I said before, resource extraction is necessary, but we must take care to look after the environment while doing so.

"Your actions have also awakened willingness in others to look at things differently. When they saw that The Coalition could be convinced to help when the evacuation after the earthquake was needed, they realized that they did not have to sit complacently while their world was shattered around them. And for that I commend you.

"I believe that in the future it will be necessary for our country to become self-sufficient in providing food for citizens and to become wholly resource independent of all other nations. As I see it, that is the only way we will ever free ourselves from the shackles of the world monetary system. That will also free us from having to give away our ideals in order to compete in a scheme where there are truly no winners. Once we can look after ourselves, we will be in the position to help others.

"The environmental damage that has been done here in our rush to compete on the world markets has been extensive. The water that was once pure and clear has been adulterated. The recent earthquake has changed the lay of the land and the flow of the drainage systems. There is nothing we can do to correct those things.

"On a positive note, given time, the earth will heal herself and the waters will run clean again. The birds and animals will return and the lush forests will regrow. This is all dependent, however, on mankind allowing the process to take place without interference. It comes back to ensuring minimal intrusion in order to retrieve those things that we need.

"Stay true to each other, my friends. Support each other. Love each other. I wish you and all future generations all the happiness and joy that this life can bring."

They spent the rest of the afternoon visiting and laughing with each other. After a while, Landon took Nora by the hand and they stepped outdoors. Bob padded silently behind them.

The pale bluish gray of dusk was settling in over the treetops to the east as the bright orange sky to the west showered the hillsides in its glow.

Landon put his arm around Nora's shoulder as she stepped in close to him. They stood together with Bob by their side and watched the sun setting, each silently hoping that they were at the beginning of better times.

Their solitude was broken as a black, dragonfly-shaped object rose above the mountains to the south. It hovered, blades chopping at the air, and then roared past them, directly over Charles's property. A glint of golden sunlight was seen reflecting off the lens in its underbelly.

Its prey could only sit and watch.

§§§

Epilogue

Shortly after the Tintina Trench earthquake, Wolfgang Grimm was removed from Yukon and transferred to Vancouver where he was appointed Vice-President, International Public Relations. Mahalia accompanied him as his executive assistant.

Sam Chong was recalled to The Capitol, and subsequently reassigned to Vancouver Island to deal with dissidents that had begun to gather there.

The charges against Melody Lloyd and Josef Poste never did come to trial. Both were granted a stay-of-proceedings. Lloyd was sent to South America by her company to oversee a mine there and Poste was given a position in the militia in the Maritime region.

Tom Alexander was never heard from again.

The Coalition had protected its own.

It was another seven years before *The Agreement* expired. During that time many mines in the wilderness areas continued practices that were damaging to habitat, watersheds and other areas of the environment. Oil and gas exploration came to a virtual standstill while the causes, if any, of the massive earthquake were investigated.

When *The Agreement* lapsed in 2043, a pseudo federal election was held. The Coalition was its overseer. When the new Government of Canada took over, it was saddled with the debt that Canada owed to The Coalition, and therefore continued having its hands tied while The Coalition pulled the strings.

Parliament began the painstaking task of creating an electoral method that was designed to make sure that the elected officials truly represented the majority of the country's citizens and protected the minorities. There has been much bickering and very little cooperation in that effort.

The requirement to purchase potable water from The Coalition-approved sources continued with The Coalition and the government still being unable to ascertain that the groundwater would be safe for drinking. In some remote locations, such as the small stream that Landon McGuire had discovered, the years had purified the flow. Each year, more of these locales were found; however, it was still illegal to draw water from them.

The issues with The Coalition were not limited to Yukon. The quest for resources was rife with complications across the country.

In neighbouring British Columbia, late in 2036, the pipeline that had been built from Brudenheim, Alberta to Kitimat, B.C. earlier in the century burst in two locations as a result of the further shifting of the earth's plates that began in the Tintina Trench and carried on through the Rocky Mountain Trench. Millions of gallons of crude oil and condensate desolated the landscape across northern B.C.

The MV Prince Rupert, a 400-metre long, mammoth ultra-large crude carrier with a payload of 550,000 deadweight tonnage, was grounded in one of the small passages south of Kitimat, B.C. during the summer of 2041. Within hours, the hull cracked open and crude oil poured into the sea, covering the shoreline on both sides. An untold amount of the sludge sank to lower depths as it moved southward. By September of that year, the eastern shoreline of Vancouver Island and the west coast of B.C. were covered in black, viscous muck. Millions of shorebirds, fish and mammals of all species perished as a result.

The governments of British Columbia and of Canada began the time-consuming, expensive cleanup process. The corporations responsible for the mishaps were taken to court; however, five years later, there was still no conclusion and the citizens of Canada were left paying the expenses—a continuum of what had taken place since as far back as the ill-fated Exxon Valdez in 1989.

Geo-mapping that had been completed from 2014–2020 uncovered a quantum amount of hidden resources in Canada's north. Billions of barrels of oil, trillions of cubic feet of natural gas and untold wealth in precious metals were revealed.

Despite nation-wide escalated confrontations, the corporate behemoths have continued to push for ever-increasing profits.

§§§

Norm Hamilton

I hope you enjoyed this story as much as I appreciated creating it. It was formed from the rich amalgam of my experiences, observations, fears, fantasies and imagination. The medley of characters presented themselves as the story unfolded, each with their own part to play in its narrative.

The extraction of oil and gas, and the mining of mineral resources are necessary in today's world. However, I urge that we rethink the importance we place on removing it as quickly as possible in our quest for the monetary riches and start placing more emphasis on protecting the environment so these industries can continue to provide the comfort and ease of life they offer without causing further harm.

Norm Hamilton
www.normhamilton.ca/writer
norm@normhamilton.ca

If you purchased this book from Amazon, please take the time to return and leave a review. I'd love to hear your thoughts.

About the Author

Norm Hamilton (1951-) lived in Whitehorse, Yukon for 40 years and is currently on Vancouver Island with his wife, Anna, where he is meeting people and experiencing new adventures to write about. He is a photographer and freelance writer. He is currently enjoying Lake Cowichan, B.C.

A skilled photographer, Norm also has a non-fiction book, "The Digital Eye," a compilation of articles for people wanting to improve their photography skills.

www.ingramcontent.com/pod-product-compliance
Lightning Source LLC
Chambersburg PA
CBHW071144170626
46809CB00002B/758